Island Charms

Sharon McGregor

Whimsical Publications, LLC

Florida

Island Charms is a work of fiction. Names, characters, and incidents are the products of the author's imagination and are either fictitious or are used fictitiously. Any resemblance to actual events or persons, living or dead, is entirely coincidental.

If you purchased this book without a cover, you should be aware that this book may have been stolen property and reported as "unsold and destroyed" to the publisher. In such case, neither the publisher nor the author has received payment for this "stripped book."

To purchase the authorized electronic edition of *Island Charms*, visit www.whimsicalpublications.com

Cover art by Traci Markou
Editing by Brieanna Robertson

ISBN-13: 978-1-940707-36-5

Published by
Whimsical Publications, LLC
Florida

Chapter One

Abby had just pulled on her gardening gloves and was trying to escape into the backyard without Ajax, her intuitive tabby cat. She knew once he got outside, she'd have to search for him for hours to herd him back inside. In his kittenhood, Ajax had been an outdoor cat, but Abby had convinced him for the most part that his ears and the rest of him stayed much healthier when he only chased birds and other cats through the closed window pane.

The phone shrilled at her from the hallway just as she was about to slip out. She considered ignoring it, but in her experience, avoided calls had to be dealt with eventually; might as well do it now. Besides, she was hoping for a call from her son Matthew.

She answered and was greeted with a quick response. "Abby, I need you to come out to the lake this week. It's really important. It's about the book I e-mailed you the information on—the one you'll ghostwrite for me about Bret."

It took a moment for Abby to place the voice.

"Nikki!" She finally got it. There had been no e-mail from Nikki when she'd checked this morning. Either she'd missed it in the flood of spam, or it was still waiting for her. It was ages since she'd last heard from Nikki. Probably not since the annual Christmas cards.

"Abby, haven't you been listening?"

Of course, Abby thought, only Nicki would find it absurd that someone she hadn't talked to for years didn't recognize her voice straight away.

"I've got the arrangements all settled. You won't have to do a thing except come." Then her voice took on an unaccustomed pleading undertone. "Please come, Abby. I need you."

"To write Bret's biography?" At least that was what she assumed Nikki was saying. Without reading the e-mail, it was difficult to interpret just what Nikki was getting at. "Nikki, you know it's not the type of work I do. And I don't ghostwrite. I don't understand why you want to do this; I thought you were trying to escape public scrutiny."

"Well, you can do it your way then; we'll work out the details. I want to let people know how Bret's life really was, not the version that hit the tabloids. Just come. All the people you need to talk to will be right there. We're having a family retreat."

"On Bret's Island? The one on Lake of the Woods? I thought you didn't like it there."

"We're regrouping. It's been a rather unfortunate year for the family."

That was an understatement. Nikki's husband Bret Cummings had been a mining mogul, a jet-setter, and the paparazzi's darling. Along with his photogenic wife, they had graced a few front pages and taken up many inches of space in the gossip columns. His affairs, her affairs, or not, depending on who you believed. Then his empire began to run into troubles—mergers and talks of mergers, overextensions and takeover bids. They had all been gloated over in the news. In January, Bret had been on a bush plane on the way to a northern Manitoba mining site when the plane had run into trouble. It had taken days to find the wreckage and the bodies of Bret, his long-time friend Josh Baranoski, and the pilot. They had died on impact, but rumors had circulated. All the family linen had been rewashed in public. It hadn't helped that Nikki had remarried so quickly.

"Abby? We're going to be on the island this coming Friday. I'll send you an itinerary and tickets. You'll fly to Kenora and..."

"I'll let you know."

"What?" The idea of a refusal hadn't entered Nikki's consciousness. "But, Abby..."

Tom had knelt beside Bronco and, turning to the others, pointed to an object lying beside the dead man. Even from where she stood, Abby could see that it was a syringe. She remembered Nikki's comments about Bronco's former drug habit. Why would a man who had been clean, for years apparently, suddenly start using again? And why an overdose?

Brady made a move to the door. "We need to call the emergency services," he said. "I'll call them. I think we'd better not do anything until they get here."

"Let's get Irene out of here," said Abby. She helped Tracy guide the stricken woman to the lounge. Since Tracy seemed to have more of a rapport with Irene than she did, Abby decided to leave her to do the comforting. "I'll make some coffee," she said. "Or maybe tea would be better." They always said strong tea with sugar was good for shock, and Irene was in need of something.

Kara was coming down the stairs as Abby crossed back to the kitchen. "What's going on?" she said, stifling back a yawn. "Sounded like bloody murder. It woke me up." She said the latter accusingly, looking at Abby, who was the closest to her to assign the blame.

"Go back to bed, Kara. I'm afraid Bronco has had an accident." Accident? Was that what you called an overdose? "There's nothing you can do to help now. Someone is looking after Irene and the authorities are on their way. Go back to bed."

"Is he dead?"

"Yes, I'm afraid so."

"Well, then." Kara turned and went back up the stairs. Abby felt a little shocked by her apparent lack of feeling, but then teenagers had a different perspective on life and sometimes hadn't developed the necessary mechanisms for displaying empathy. She shook the feeling off. Aside from Irene, maybe no one would feel Bronco's death deeply.

Tom, Neil, Nikki, and Jill sat around the kitchen table, silent and expressionless. Abby put the kettle on for tea and set up the percolator as well. Then she sat at the table with the others.

"Did you know Bronco was back on drugs?" she asked Nikki.

"No! You don't think I'd allow him on the place if he was, do you? Especially not with Kara here." She suddenly realized her daughter was not with them. "I'd better go find her," she said.

"It's okay," said Abby. "I met her on the stairs and sent her back to bed."

"Does she know what's going on?'

"I told her. She's better off upstairs."

Abby took the boiling water and poured it into the large teapot. The percolator was bubbling in its final stages of brewing. "Will they send a plane or a boat?" she asked.

"Probably a boat," said Tom. "The police will be coming, as well as the doctor."

Brady reappeared. "They're on their way," he said. "They asked about the circumstances, so I told them about the syringe. They said be sure not to touch anything."

"A little late for that."

Tracy poked her head around the door. "I'm taking Irene to her room. She wants to go with the emergency services when they take the bo—Bronco. I hope they let her?"

"If not, we'll take her in our boat," said Nikki.

"Right. I'm going to pack her things. I don't imagine she's going to want to come back here."

They began to wander away from the kitchen. Abby walked out the back door to the garden yard. She noticed a small scrap of paper and stooped idly to pick it up. It was a candy bar wrapper—Caramilk, the same kind she had seen in the cabin. Was Bronco the one who had been using the cabin? Maybe he needed a private place to keep and ingest his drugs. She thought back to her few run-ins with Bronco. He hadn't given the appearance of someone on drugs. Surly, unfriendly, a little frightening, perhaps, but definitely someone who seemed to be functioning in the real world. She remembered his hand as he'd grazed past her in the doorway—steady and firm.

She shifted her gaze from the Caramilk wrapper and looked toward the trees. A sudden flutter of color in the bushes made her jump. Who could be in the trees? Abby was sure she had seen a flash of material, not an animal coat. Besides, it was too high from the ground to be a skunk or martin, or whatever small animals inhabited the island, and it definitely wasn't a bird. She started forward, but reason advised caution. Besides, everyone on the island was accounted for and in the house. She decided to double check.

"I'll let you know," she said firmly, more firmly than she had ever been with Nikki. The troubles she had ended up in at college because she hadn't been able to say no firmly enough to Nikki still made her shudder. She remembered the impromptu marshmallow roast they'd had behind the res one night. Nikki had thought it a great idea and they'd all agreed. They'd made the bonfire too close to some shrubbery and needed help to put the fire out, so they'd run across to the men's residence for help. By the time it was out, a crowd had gathered, including the dean of women's res. Naturally, Nikki had gone home by then and missed the scathing talk they'd received. She was the only one of the four friends that didn't live in residence. Then there was the time...well, there were a lot of times. Of course, Nikki had always walked away from situations as the shining girl. That wasn't going to start again.

Chapter Two

Abby looked down at the phone she was still holding and hung up, knowing she wasn't even going to consider the proposition. She'd rehearse her refusal, stiffen her spine with a double rum, and call back tomorrow. She had made great progress, she felt, even suggesting noncompliance to Nikki. Of course it was easier to say no to Nikki on the phone. Face to face, she'd probably revert to old behaviors and cave in to whatever Nikki wanted. They always had, the small group of college friends.

Abby released the cradled phone, trying to reground herself into the present. She dropped her gardening gloves on the hall table, all plans for weeding now on hold. She wandered into the living room and sat down in the burgundy easy chair, leaning back to enjoy its outdated comfort. Her living room was not large, and an interior decorator would call it cluttered, amongst other things, but it had nearly thirty years of history in it and she had always felt protected in this room, even during the worst days when she and Richard divorced.

She got up and strolled over to the piano in the corner, running her fingers gently over the keys. She didn't really play, just plunked away when she thought no one was listening. Matthew, her son, was the pianist. She missed him and wondered what comforts he was doing without. Matthew was a nurse and worked through Doctors Without Borders in some difficult parts of the world. She was very proud of her son, but missed him terribly and feared for his safety every time she listened to the news and heard of turmoil where he was working. He would be here for a short while next month, just in time to celebrate his birthday. She'd hoped when the phone rang, he was calling to say he'd be home earlier than planned.

Now that should create some fun, she thought, trying to coordinate celebrations with both parents, as well as old friends. Richard's current bimbo—ouch had she really said that, even to herself—probably had some spectacular to-do planned, but Abby would hold out for a private, smaller celebration. Probably the only way to go was to have two separate parties. Then everyone would be happy. She was glad Mandy was home for the summer. She always seemed to ride shotgun between family members. She would have done great as a diplomat, thought Abby. Who would have ever predicted she'd end up studying to be a vet? She would have pictured Matthew the more likely candidate for vet and Mandy to be the globe-trotter, but kids always surprised you. Anyhow, she had enough family activity planned that she would be able to make an easy excuse to Nikki. She just needed time to rehearse.

The old Westminster chimed a quarter hour and Abby jumped. Time to reminisce and think about Nikki later.

For now, she had other things to think of—dinner for instance. Tony was due at six-thirty and she hadn't even done the shopping yet. Abby didn't feel at home in the kitchen. Throughout her marriage to Richard, the kitchen was his domain, the garden hers. It wasn't as though Tony was a gourmet; he just held a few old-fashioned ideas about women and kitchens and had expressed wonder on several occasions that she had never cooked a meal for him. Something simple was called for. She considered spaghetti Bolognese, but she hadn't yet reached the comfort level with Tony where she could picture herself dangling wayward spaghetti with him. Too bad, she always considered there was an inherent romanticism to spaghetti—probably too many viewings of Lady and The Tramp. Oriental stir fry; that would be easy to make and not the type of food to jump up and ambush you like spaghetti, as long as there were no chopsticks, and there were definitely not going to be chopsticks.

She grabbed her purse and keys, shooed Ajax away from the open front door, and headed for the store.

She went to the meat department first and picked up a package of stir fry sirloin, then off to the vegetables for sugar snap peas, broccoli, and bell peppers. She checked the recipe mentally. Onion and garlic she had. She bought a bottle of sesame ginger stir fry sauce. When she got home, she'd decant it into a container and throw away the bottle. Tony might suspect a store bought sauce, but he was much too well-mannered to suggest the possibility. She made one last stop at the liquor store. She had some Merlot at home, but she knew Tony preferred Shiraz, so she picked up a bottle of Australian.

She laid the ingredients out, hiding the beef from Ajax's inquiring senses and, grabbing a basket and scissors at the back door, wandered into her garden. A back corner was reserved for vegetables. She ignored the places where her weeding was slipping; there was portulaca growing between the rows of peas. It was so difficult to keep out of a garden once it gained a foothold; pull out one bunch and the roots crawled underground to sprout up somewhere else. Oh well. No time for weeding now. She'd just blame Nikki for that. She picked over the lettuce; it was getting a little old even though she kept topping it, but she found some nice leaves to add to the red leaf she bought from the store. The spinach also was past the days of tiny salad shoots, but she gathered some of the smaller leaves. Radishes were definitely done; the summer heat had turned the remainder woody, but she had bell peppers in the fridge for color, so she just needed some green onions and a small carrot or two.

Should she chance some flowers for the table? She glanced back at the door to see Ajax watching her with an innocent expression, which she knew from experience was when you doubted him most. For some reason, he had a passion for cut flowers, especially sweet peas and baby's breath. He'd nibble at them, and invariably knock the vase sideways. She'd risk it. She'd just hide the flowers in the bathroom until Tony came. She knew Ajax would make himself scarce then and not come out till he had left. He was not a Tony fan. Abby didn't know if she should read something into that or not. Cats had weird fancies. Look at how they would enter a room full of people and make straight for the one who hated them or was allergic. Abby thought maybe it was a power play. Sweet peas were her favorite flower. She loved the heady scent they gave off and the variety of colors in her Spencer Mixed. They were just starting to bloom nicely now. They'd had an early start this year.

Back inside, she washed the salad veggies and left them to drain, then locked the flower vase in the bathroom and went to change.

She pulled on a plain grey skirt and topped it with a soft teal blouse with sleeves that ended just below the elbow. She would have felt more comfortable in slacks and a top or a pants suit, but Tony liked to see her in a skirt, so she decided to make the effort. She turned from side to side in the long mirror and examined herself critically. The blouse seemed to bulge slightly over the waist and the skirt was definitely no larger around the hips than need be, but overall, not too bad. Her legs were long and not fallen to flab or too much cellulite around the thighs yet. They could do with a little color, though. Abby hadn't had much time to laze around in the sun this summer.

She swiped on some blush and a touch of liner on her eyes. She always felt her face was rather bland and needed some added definition, but the art was beyond her. Besides, with her fiftieth birthday looming in the near distance, she knew gobs of eye shadow and rings of kohl were not the answer. A touch of lipstick would have to do the defining for now. Her dark brown straight hair fell to the bottom of her earlobes and she brushed a few stray hairs from her cheek. She wished she had her daughter's eyes. Mandy had inherited her father's bright blue irises, fortunately for her, rather than what Abby considered her unremarkable hazel.

Shoes! What was she going to wear for shoes? Something with a strap—good for making the ankles look smaller. She pulled on a pair of low heels; most of her shoes were. She was five-eight, not exactly Amazon, but still, she felt safer somehow in low heels. A quick look at her watch made her throw down her hairbrush and make a run for the stairs. She'd barely have time to get her ingredients sorted.

Chapter Three

Dinner preparations were nearly done when the doorbell rang. In spite of the months they had been seeing each other, no suggestion had been made on either side to exchange house keys. For her part, Abby wanted to keep her family in a different life compartment from her social side. Mandy had met Tony, but Abby could tell she was unimpressed. She had probably discussed him with Matthew and Richard, but the fewer times their paths crossed, the better. At least until she knew where she stood with Tony. She didn't really want to speculate on his reasons for the degree of separation.

Tony followed her to the kitchen and curled his arms around her waist, resting his chin on her shoulder. He was not a tall man and didn't have to stoop much. He was only a couple of inches taller than Abby when she wore her low heels. "Mmm. Beef stir fry? Nice." He released her and went to pour the wine.

Abby turned sharply to examine his expression after the lukewarm "nice," but didn't have the time or inclination to decipher the nuances of the comment. Maybe she was imagining it. Why did she have herself so worked up over this dinner? She wasn't auditioning for Cordon Bleu, although Tony was probably just as difficult to impress.

Dinner passed uneventfully with small talk about his work, her work, and a movie they both wanted to see. He cleared the table and she stacked the dishwasher. Tony made himself at home in her kitchen, a fact that pleased her at the same time as it unsettled her, since kitchens had never been her home turf. She felt awkward under his watch, watching for facial expressions that might condemn her imperfect housekeeping. He moved around the room efficiently and smoothly, in a way that reminded her of Ajax.

It wasn't until they lay in bed, sweat damp and quiet, that he mentioned his out of town trip.

"It's a necessary evil, I'm afraid. Someone has to go, and since Edgar's wife has been sick lately, it's down to me."

Abby rolled over to look at his face. This conference was news to her. "How long will you be gone?"

"I'll be gone for the week. Probably back on Friday. It depends on connections. I might stop in Winnipeg for the night before coming home. Actually, I might spend the whole weekend. I have a friend there who'll probably be at the conference, too."

"What sort of a conference is it? You never mentioned it before." She tried to keep her voice casual, but if she could hear the whining tone, so could Tony.

"Not a very interesting one." He turned to spoon her and kissed the back of her neck. "Just necessary to put in an appearance."

"A whole week is a little more than an appearance." Ouch. Now she was beginning to sound downright shrewish.

He slid to an upright position and began to put on his socks. She was momentarily distracted by this phenomenon. Tony was the only man she had ever known to pull his socks on before his underwear and trousers. It was not a libido-arousing picture. She thought with a giggle that it was a good idea he didn't do the reverse and take his socks off last. There was nothing remotely sexy about a naked man clad only in socks.

Tony never stayed the night. He told her with a laugh on their first night together that once she had heard him snore, the romance would be gone. She would have gladly put up with a snore or two for the intimacy of awakening to a shared bed. But then, she couldn't complain about Tony's arm-length measures; she was guilty too. Much as she would like to awaken to the smell of coffee and Tony in the kitchen, she would experience a strange sense of calm when he made his exit, like the exhale of relief after finishing a gruelling test. What did that say about their relationship?

When he had gone, she sat at the kitchen table drinking the dregs of the wine bottle. She realized Tony had never even told her where the conference was. She didn't know if it was in Tallahassee or Edmonton.

Next morning, she was still thinking about Tony and his out of town trip. Abby knew she had issues of self-confidence where men were concerned, but her restless mind turned things over and over. She was probably overcompensating now for her lack of suspicion during her marriage to Richard. She knew very little about Tony's life where it didn't touch hers other than the fact that he was a pharmacist at a local clinic. He didn't encourage her to drop in there. As a matter of fact, he didn't encourage her to infringe on any of his life outside of their own relationship. She began to imagine some scenarios that she knew wouldn't leave her mind until she had the question resolved. When Tony came back, they were going to have to talk. They both needed clarification.

She came to a quick decision and acted before she could change her mind. She was between projects and knew if she stayed here, she would spend the next week working herself up into a state about her relationship with Tony and wondering where the hell he was and if he would call. She needed a distraction. Besides, it would be fun to relive some of the good old days with a college chum, maybe even some of the not so good old days. They always talked about having a group reunion, but never got around to it. Maybe if this week with Nikki went well, they could set up a weekend at the island with the rest of the old crew. Somehow, after being so close in college, their lives had taken them to different parts of the continent, nostalgia holding them together with Christmas letters and e-mails.

Chapter Four

Nikki didn't answer, but her message machine beeped promisingly. "Hi, Nikki. It's Abby. I've thought it over and decided to take you up on your offer. No promises about doing the actual project, but I'll listen to what you have to say and we can have a good visit if nothing else. Please send your itinerary and location."

She had barely hung up the phone when the doorbell rang. She opened it to a courier who stood there with a pen in hand. She glanced at the information on the letter packet. Just like Nikki. She never considered for a moment that Abby was going to refuse to come when she called. No one ever did.

She signed for the delivery, threw it on the kitchen table, and sighed, pouring a second cup of coffee before opening the envelope. Out came an airline ticket to Kenora, maps and information detailing the time she would be met at the airport and then taken to the marina in Kenora to be flown by pontoon plane to the island. Also included were dramatis personae. A note written in large, upright letters in purple ink scrawled the words, "You'll find enclosed the list of everyone who will be on the island. I've got an information packet on each, which you may find interesting. It will be ready when you arrive. As soon as you get here—Nikki had underscored it with a no-nonsense brooked line—I need to talk to you. We'll slip away somewhere private. Thanks for coming, Abby."

Very curious. Why did Nikki feel the need to provide a dossier on all her guests? And why not include it in the package if it was that important? She obviously wanted to talk to Abby before she read the dossiers, but why? Abby knew there was a lot more to this than writing a biography of Bret, if that was even an item in the equation. She knew in her gut she was going to regret this trip; nothing connected to Nikki was ever simple or easy. She considered reneging, but she was already committed by her phone call, and her innate curiosity wouldn't let her back out. In college, she had been nicknamed Abby the Cat because she could never let a mystery go unsolved, even if it was just why Steven Cramer always came to class with mismatched socks. The prosaic answer had been that he was color blind, but Abby never rested until she found the reason.

Ajax came to wind himself around her ankles, giving plaintive little mews. They would get much louder if she didn't fill his food dish straight away. As she opened the can and dumped half of it into his bowl, she began to plan her trip. Clothes were iffy. It was summer, which called for shorts and tees, a bathing suit, and casual slacks. However, this was an island out in Lake of the Woods. Nights would probably get chilly, so sweaters would be needed. Also, she'd be rubbing shoulders with people who shopped in swankier places than she could afford. The heck with that; comfort was called for and she'd pack accordingly.

"Ajax," she said out loud. Ajax didn't reply; he had better manners than to talk with his mouth full. She'd have to call Mandy to be sure she could come over a couple of times a day to feed him. Her daughter Mandy was enrolled in a veterinarian college in Saskatoon, but was off for the summer interning with a local vet. Instead of staying with either her mother or father, she elected to stay with her old college roommate for the summer. Abby hoped it was just a declaration of independence, not evidence of a lifestyle her parents wouldn't approve of. *Give your head a shake, Abby,* she thought. *Mandy is twenty-two years old and quite capable of looking after herself.* Her glorious days of teenage rebellion were behind her.

"Mandy?" It took five rings to get an answer.

"Hi, Mom. Go away. Shoo. Not you, Mom. We're trying to corral the mosquito market here. The citronella candles just aren't cutting it."

"Have you tried a bug zapper? They usually do the trick."

"Not on the budget, I'm afraid. What's up with you?"

"How would you like to be Ajax's minder for a week?"

"You're going away? Great." There was a loud slap, sounded as though at least one of Manitoba's provincial birds had bit the dust. "Sorry, didn't mean it to come out that way. I just meant it's nice you're taking a holiday. Anyone I know?" Abby could hear her attempt at a leer.

"Not that kind of going away."

"Tony not into romantic getaways?"

"I don't know about the romantic, but Tony's going to be away on a pharmaceutical convention all next week."

"And you're going with him for company? Sounds nice." Her voice didn't echo the sentiment. Abby knew Mandy wasn't fond of Tony, probably a normal reaction toward her mother's boyfriend. She wasn't sure how Mandy felt about Richard's current lady, Kelly. She never talked about her, which Abby took as a good sign. It probably meant she didn't discuss Tony with Richard. But then, why should she care what her ex-husband thought?

"No. He's going alone. This is something different. I'm actually off to a retreat on an island on Lake of the Woods. Not to retreat, more to talk over possibilities for an 'as told to.' You remember me talking about Nikki, my old college friend?"

"Oh yes, the one who could walk on water and not get wet."

"Ouch. Is that how I made her sound? There's a little more to her than that. Anyhow, she's invited me to stay for the week and I need someone to come over twice a day to look after Ajax. Can you manage it?"

"Of course. Look, Mom, why don't I just come and stay while you're gone? It would make things easier, and Ajax would be a lot less inclined toward revenge when you get back if he has company."

Abby read a little more into the "make things easier" than Mandy probably intended.

"Roommate problems?" she asked.

"The roommate isn't the problem," Mandy sighed. "Jess is wonderful and still my best friend. It's her new boyfriend I can't stand. My tongue is nearly severed from biting it when he's around, which is nearly all the time. I think we'll all breathe a little easier if I get away for a week. When are you going?"

"Day after tomorrow. How's the job going?"

"Fantastic." The joy was back in her voice. "Yesterday, I went along for the delivery of twin kids."

"I thought lambing season, or kidding, I guess it would be, was in spring."

"It is, usually. This was a mistake. Goat hormones running amok out of season or something. The delivery was a bit awkward, but great training for me, and everything turned out okay in the end." Another slap, another mosquito bit the dust. "I'm going back inside. What time do you want me?"

"I'm leaving around noon, but if you can't make it by then, you've still got the key, haven't you?"

"Don't worry, Mom, I haven't flown that far from the nest yet. I still have the key."

"There's lots of cat food here and another bag of kitty litter in the garage. Oh, and don't forget to give the plants some water. The flower beds too, and the lawn. I guess it would be asking too much to give it a mow? I should have done it yesterday, but..." Abby broke off. She wasn't going to admit to her daughter that worrying about something as simple as cooking dinner for Tony got in the way of her yard duties.

"Slave-driver. Not promising about the mowing, but I'll look after everything else. Give me a call some night."

"That might be a problem. The island is isolated. As far as I know, there's no phone and probably no Internet either. I'll take along my cell and see if it works, but don't be surprised if you don't hear from me till I'm home."

"Well, I hope you have a nice, peaceful stay, but if Nikki is anything like your stories, I rather doubt it.'

So do I, thought Abby as she hung up the phone. *So do I.*

Chapter
Five

Nikki picked up her coffee mug, the purple one with the Charms logo on it, and took a slow sip after first sniffing the contents. That bit of prudence had become a habit now. *Maybe the police detective was right*, she thought. *Maybe I am getting paranoid.* Then she thought again of that near miss on the winding road going out and shivered. *I'm not paranoid; the danger is real.* She wondered if Abby had received the Purolator package yet. Abby had said, "I'll let you know." But Nikki knew she'd come. Abby had always said that. She didn't like to jump into things, and always left herself a way out, but she never took it.

It had been the same all the way through college. Nikki and Jessica had been the innovators, the ones who came up with the ideas. Abby took her time, but usually came around. Then they all worked together on Summer. She was always the cautious one. Nikki sighed. For all the trouble they managed to get into, life had been so simple then. The main worries were trying to think up new excuses to cut class, or finding a way around curfew, or figuring out what to wear to the class party. Kids now didn't have to worry about half those things. Now dorms were co-ed and nobody cared if you had visitors. Or what time you came and went. No nosy women's dean to monitor your social life and pass on information to your parents. Not that Nikki had worried much about the dean. She hadn't lived in res like the other three, but she spent a lot of time there.

Nikki wandered around the morning room, sipping at her cooling coffee. She looked out at the hedged garden and could see Bronco working on a terraced flower bed that sloped away from the house. His back was to her and, even though it was still cool, he was working without a shirt. She watched him for a moment, his muscular strength obvious from even this distance, and she frowned into her coffee mug. A soft breeze came in through the open screen. It wouldn't last; the forecast said hot again today, 32 degrees Celsius, feeling like 38 with humidity. Thankfully, it would be cooler on the lake. She lifted the cover on an easel and examined the painting she'd started last week. The drive to finish it had left her. She had more immediate concerns.

Nikki wandered into the kitchen to consult Irene over dinner. She felt aimless today, at loose ends not just for the present, but for her whole life, which seemed to be taking turns she hadn't planned on. This didn't please Nikki because she was used to being in the director's chair. But real life was taking some unexpected twists and unfortunately, you couldn't do retakes.

Her housekeeper was examining the contents of the crisper drawers and cleaning the fridge. She immediately straightened when Nikki came into the room. Nikki sat down at the long, benched kitchen table. As she set her coffee down, Irene made a motion toward the percolator, but Nikki shook her head.

"I wanted to talk about dinner tonight. It will be only Daniel, Kara, and me," she said. "I think it's going to be a hot day, so just leave us some cold cuts and salad and you can go home early. Bronco might as well go too. It will be too hot to do much outside work today."

Irene gave her a quick look, but agreed easily. Nikki was glad of any excuse to have Bronco off the premises. She really should fire him, but she didn't have a solid reason. She couldn't just say, "You make me nervous." Besides, Irene was too valuable to lose and they came as a pair. Whatever had Irene seen in him to want to share a life with him? And what had Bret seen in Bronco to want him as an employee?

She got up from the table and jumped as she felt an arm cross in front of her chest. "Boy, are you jumpy," said Daniel, who had come in from the hallway.

"Sorry." She turned to give her husband a kiss on the cheek and then lingered to change it to a proper one. She pulled back and examined him critically; he looked back with an amused grin.

She knew Daniel didn't mind the scrutiny. He rarely indulged in self-doubt or worried about what other people thought of him. They were wasteful pursuits. He would be examining the image in front of him, too. Nikki might be a few years older than him, but she knew she was aging well. A few laugh lines and, this morning in the mirror, she had noticed slight pouches under her eyes. Other than that, she could be taken for a much younger woman. Her dark blonde hair was cut to the bottom of her jaw and framed her face perfectly. Her blue eyes were clear and beautiful. She didn't make the mistake many older women did and gunk up her eyes with makeup. Hers was always understated and applied expertly. Nikki hadn't gained an ounce since she'd first met Daniel and made a good advertisement for their chain of fitness outlets. Still, the pouches were there, and in a few years, their age differences would be noticeable. Nikki thought her hold on Daniel was enough to compensate for minor imperfections. She didn't want to look too far into the future.

He pulled back first. "Too much caffeine," he said. "You just about went through the roof."

"You surprised me, that's all."

"I was booking for Vancouver online. My flight leaves tomorrow afternoon around three."

"Can't you put it off? I'd really like you to come with us to the island." Nikki knew it was going to be a tough week, and having her husband along could bring some welcome distraction. On the other hand, with the pressing family business on the agenda, not to mention her other worries, maybe this way was better after all.

"I wish I could, but duty calls, and my boss is a slavedriver." He grinned and perched on the edge of the table. "I should get things sorted out fairly easily. Just growing pains with a new manager."

"I still don't understand why Jonas left so suddenly. He was always so reliable. And this new manager—problems already?"

"I guess someone made Jonas an offer too good to turn

down. As for the new manager, it's probably just growing pains. I should be able to get things organized. It's just a matter of being there in person to give her some encouragement."

"Her? I thought the new manager was Doug Lewinski."

"Nope. He was short-listed, but had another offer, and I went down the list to Amanda."

"Well, sort it out as quickly as you can. Maybe you can join us later." Nikki was slightly annoyed that she had to ask Daniel to keep her updated on their business outlets. She usually kept on top of everything, but with her recent distractions, she had given Daniel his head in making management decisions. She wasn't sure if it was a good idea, but then he had to have some responsibility if he was to stay interested. She knew Daniel had a short attention span.

"I'll try." Daniel edged between Irene and the fridge and stood, looking at its contents for a few moments before pulling out a bottle of water. Irene stood watching him, hands on her hips, until he closed the door. Then she reopened the door and went back to her cleaning. Daniel took his water and headed for the back door. "I think I'll see how Bronco is getting on."

Nikki could see Irene's shoulders tense and wondered about the strain she sensed in her housekeeper whenever Daniel was present. On his part, he seemed to act as if Irene didn't exist, like the way he'd brushed past her without a glance at the fridge. She sighed. There were too many nuances present in the behavior of her household. Best not to worry about them.

She looked up at the sound of footsteps as Kara walked into the kitchen, still in her tee she wore as a nightshirt—the one sporting the slogan, "Bad Girls Don't Apologize." Her dark hair sprouted magenta streaks and stood in an unbrushed cloud around her face. Without the overstated makeup she usually wore, her face had a more youthful, vulnerable look, and Nikki felt a flashback to better times, when she and Kara and Bret had been a happy family. Well, reasonably happy. Of course they had problems, even then; everyone did.

Kara ignored Nikki and went straight to the coffee pot. She poured a cup and liberally added the cream and sugar before sitting down at the opposite end of the table. She still hadn't made eye contact.

"Are you just about packed for the island?"

"I don't want to go," Kara answered sullenly. She took a sip of her coffee, made a face, and reached for the sugar bowl again.

"It's not an option. You can't stay here alone. Besides, I want you with me."

"I don't see why. You have everyone else there."

"Everyone else isn't my daughter. You're going."

Kara picked up her coffee mug and left the room without another word. Nikki sighed and looked over to see Irene wearing an expression of sympathy. Nikki didn't want sympathy. She wanted to get her life back where it was. Back where it was before Bret died. It wasn't just losing him; everything else had changed then. Family relationships took on undertones not present before, Kara was getting out of control again, Bronco was becoming insolent. Every conversation she had now with her family meant someone was asking for something from her. She looked for hidden meanings everywhere. Even Daniel.

She could see Daniel and Bronco together in the yard. Daniel had his head thrown back in a laugh; it looked as though they were sharing a joke. Then she looked at Bronco's face and he wasn't smiling. He stood still and unmoving with a wooden expression. He must have a different sense of humor than Daniel. And now, her latest worries. Maybe Abby would be able to help sort things out. She needed an objective opinion, and Abby was the most perceptive of her friends, also the most likely to give an opinion that wasn't whitewashed in polite language.

Chapter Six

The next day, in between laundry and packing bouts, Abby made friends with Google as well as the local library and microfiche newspaper archives. Nikki said she had a dossier on the island visitors, but Abby had learned to be wary of other people's research, especially when they might have their own axe to grind. Not even knowing what Nikki had in mind for her, she felt that prudence dictated she be as forearmed as possible. From Nikki's conversation, she gathered she wouldn't be able to rely on the Internet once she landed on the island.

She found a lot of information on the Cummings—Bret, Nikki, and Tom—more about their social activities than their businesses, but she was able to get some general indications of the scope of the Cummings empire. Mining interests provided the bulk, but Bret had acquired real estate holdings along the way as well as broadcasting franchises. She found very little information on Neil Templeton, Bret's long-standing legal advisor, except for an old photo and the odd clipping in some newspaper archives she was able to access. She discovered he was on Bret's payroll, having given up his private practice. Brady, Kara and Tracy were non-starters when she searched for information on them, but she found out Jill was an actress, or aspiring to be one. She didn't find reference to a large body of work, but she had apparently been in a couple of off-off Broadway shows.

She was surprised to discover that Nikki had her own little business empire. She had started with a fitness center she'd picked up cheap and expanded it into a chain of women's franchises called Charms. Nikki had remarried not that long after Bret's death, which must have caused a little consternation amongst the family. Her new husband was Daniel Akerman, and his background was in sports. She found references to his participation in tennis tournaments and then nothing. Possibly he went from player to pro? It would be a natural jumping-off point to managing fitness centers, and apparently, he was Nikki's right-hand in Charms.

The rest of her day she prepared the house for Ajax's comfort, as he got in her way wherever she went, wrapping himself around her legs and nearly upending her on more than one occasion. A cat had radar when it came to the intentions of his owner, and he knew something that could affect his wellbeing was in the air. He didn't intend to take it lightly. She made sure his litter box was clean and his favorite foods and snacks were in unlimited supply. Mandy wouldn't have much time on her hands to go shopping.

The day passed quickly, and Abby found that in spite of her apprehension, she was actually looking forward to her trip—she needed a boost of something different.

Her good feeling carried her onto the Bearskins Airlines craft that was taking her and fifteen other passengers to Kenora. She managed a quick drink before her flight took off, not enough to squash her fear of flying, but enough to make her legs actually carry her on to a vehicle that was going to leave the ground. The flight was short and she never once opened the laptop she took as carry-on. She uncurled her knuckles from the seat rests once they were airborne, content to watch the changing scenery below shifting from open fields and agriculture to rocky roads dividing stands of forest. Water was ever present, whether in small lakes or rivers.

When they landed at Kenora, she collected her luggage and began to look around for her escort that Nikki had promised. She hadn't been specific, so she didn't know who to look for, just assured her that someone would take her in hand. Little groups of tourists in shorts and sandals with cameras seemed to wander the small airport aimlessly. A tall, thin man in a suit was waving to get the attention of a pair of Oriental businessmen, and assorted family members jumped with delight into the arms of other family members.

Then she spotted him—a medium-height, wiry-looking man in khaki shorts and beige polo shirt leaned against a wall scanning the room. His dirty blond hair fell Veronica Lake style over one eye. He swiped it back with his hand and jerked his head back at the same time, bringing his gaze up to meet Abby's. Immediately, he smiled and straightened, the smile taking away the hawk-like appearance of his features. He approached her with a confident hand held out. "You must be Mrs. Addison." She nodded at his lifted eyebrow and reached to pick up her suitcase. "Yes," she said. "Abby, actually, and you're Neil Templeton?" She would never have recognized him from the blurred newspaper archive photo, but he couldn't really be anyone else.

"You've been forewarned," he said. "Here, let me take that. There's a taxi waiting to take us to the marina. We'll fly on a pontoon plane right to the island."

It was a five-mile drive to Kenora and then a quick trip to the docks where they pulled in to the marina. They spoke little during the ride, but she took the opportunity to take closer note of the more elusive of Nikki's guests. He was not a large man, but a latent power simmered beneath the surface. His movements were graceful but economical. His hair was not as blond as she had thought; there was a great deal of grey that wasn't apparent at first glance. Sensing her examination, he turned. Again, that quick smile transformed his face from the harsh, predatory look of a corporate lawyer to something nearing sensitivity. Abby wondered what he thought of being the errand boy and official escort of his employer. Not really part of his job description.

Neil paid the taxi driver and collected her suitcase. "You're a light traveler." He smiled approvingly. "There's a bench over there. Have a seat while I check on our take-off time."

He walked the length of the dock to a small high-wing plane with hatch open taking on cargo. After a few minutes conversation with the two men loading it, he returned. "We'll be leaving in just a few minutes. We won't be the only passengers. There are a couple of fishermen getting off at an island camp with their gear; then we'll be on to Cummings Island." He noticed her wince. "Nervous flyer?'

"I'm okay in regular planes," she said, stretching the truth a little. She had always been a white-knuckle flyer, but rather than let it defeat her, she had learned a few tricks to handle the fear—from meditation to the drinks cart—or at least to keep it from being obvious to others. "I've just never taken off from the water, and it looks like I'll be doing it twice."

He sat beside her on the bench. "Nothing to worry about. The weather's great and the pilot's made these runs so often he could do them blindfolded." He reached over and touched her hand, briefly but comfortingly. She gave a slight shudder at the contact, and said, "Sorry to be a nervous Nellie." But she knew the shudder had nothing to do with her fear of flying. She glanced sideways at his profile and wondered at the controlled intensity she could almost feel beneath the rather ordinary features.

A little nervous under the weight of silence, she said, "Until I started map-reading after Nikki's invitation, I hadn't realized just how big Lake of the Woods is."

"It's approximately seventy miles across both ways," he said, settling himself comfortably into the bench, "and there are over fourteen thousand islands on the lake, most of them in the Northern section." He waved a hand expansively and possessively over the lake. "The voyageurs explored this area coming from Lake Superior. They built a fort on Rainy River in 1731 and came further west as far as the lake the next year." He went on, talking as though he assumed her interest would equal his. "A few years later, LaVerendrye's nephew led a party farther west on the lake and ran into a group of Sioux who had been lying in wait for them." He glanced sideways at her as if to check her level of interest. She appreciated his attempts to divert her attention and smiled back. Satisfied, he went on. "Five days later, they found the bodies on an island near Hay Island. They had all been scalped and beheaded. They call it Massacre Island today. There's a cross erected there as a tribute. Actually, there are two islands that vie for the name. The jury's still out on which is the right one."

Even though she had started her working life as a teacher, Abby had never felt a connection to history the way Neil apparently did. But then, her subject had been Language Arts. She tried to remember the history she'd learned in school about the fur-traders. "From what I remember, history has always been a little bloodthirsty. You should have been a teacher."

"I don't think that would have worked. Faced with a room full of blank faces that would rather be playing video games or football, I'd just get annoyed."

The pilot waved at them to come along and they climbed in, followed by the two fishermen. The plane made a run across the water with ear-blowing noise and took off. Neil flashed a sympathetic smile and patted her hand again. She wondered at this electric tingle she felt every time he touched her; Tony had never, even in their first days, had this effect. She glanced over at his profile and saw a face that looked relaxed and at ease, a face she could well imagine on a southern plantation owner as he sat on his veranda drinking mint juleps. The picture was so far from what was probably the truth—a cutthroat lawyer glued to cell phone and laptop—that she had to stifle a giggle. Really, flying had a strange effect on her.

Soon they levelled off and she began to relax. Take-offs were, for Abby, the worst. Even though she knew landings were more dangerous, they didn't bother her nearly as much. She just felt happy to be going in the right direction—down. Logic never had much of a part to play in phobias.

The first leg was short and they soon landed at a dock that stood at the base of a large lodge flying Canadian, American, and a few other flags she didn't recognize. A welcoming committee came to greet the fishermen and take their baggage. Abby braced herself for the next take-off.

After a seemingly interminable time, which Abby knew was only a few minutes, Neil leaned over her to point at the water below. "There's Cummings Island. We'll be turning to make a landing in a moment." The plane banked and turned as he spoke. Abby could see the island below, long and teardrop-shaped, rather like a map of South America without the sharp point, marked by a gouge cut into one side of the big end. This was their point of entry, a tiny harbor away from the winds. A boathouse lined one side of the dock. Through the open entry, she could see the end of a canoe. A couple of rowboats and a larger boat were tied up across from the boathouse. She was too intent on their safe landing to pay much attention to the buildings along the hump from the harbor. She'd see them soon enough.

She gritted her teeth and prepared for the landing—not of the plane, but the landing into whatever intrigue Nikki was pulling her into.

Chapter
Seven

As the plane sputtered to a stop, the pilot jumped out and secured it to the dock, pulling it close enough for them to exit. Neil stepped across Abby's knees, bracing his hand against her leg as the plane gave a little settling shudder, echoing the one that slipped through her core. He got out first, and then reached out a helping hand. She didn't meet his eyes for a moment, but shook off the feeling of foolishness and gave him a quick smile of thanks. She felt a little wobbly-kneed, as she usually did after flying. Taking a deep breath, she looked around to orient herself, saw the brightly-painted red boat-house with two yellow canoe ends visible in the opening, and the other watercraft tied up to the dock. The motorboat looked much bigger from ground level—a small cabin cruiser, on closer inspection, sporting the name Nikki B in blue cursive writing. There was a flagged stone walk heading up a slight rise, circling the trees that appeared to cover most of the island. She picked out a variety of foliage—white and black poplars, certainly, and some evergreens, lots of underbrush, tall grasses with splashes of wildflower colors, and willows closer to the water. A small stream opened up over some loose stones splashing into the lake with a little gurgling sound. Partway up the rise, the cobbled path turned over the stream with a picture postcard walking bridge.

She inhaled a potpourri of scents—pine needles, lake water, composting leaves, with an underlying current of fuel fumes from the departing plane making the only sour note.

Abby turned to the lake side to watch as the plane taxied out to open water and then, with a surge of throttle, sped along the lake, churning up a large wake behind. It cleared water and began to rise, turning as it did. Her bridges were well and truly burned.

"It's just a short walk along the trail," Neil said, grabbing her suitcase. "They'll likely be gathered on the deck by the pool. I think you could do with a drink. Or maybe you'd rather grab a swim first?"

"I'll wait to see what Nikki has planned," she said. *In more ways than one*, she thought.

The trail was steeper than it looked, or Abby was more out of shape than she thought. In either case, she was panting slightly by the time they reached the compound. There were some outbuildings to the left; she expected the power came from a generator and there'd be supply sheds as well. The house rose rather grandly to her right, three stories high, although the top story with its tiny windows was probably attic and storerooms. The natural wood finish seemed to blend in with the surroundings as well as you could expect a mansion to blend into a wilderness. A deck ran around the sides she could see, railed at the two sides but open at the front except for supporting white pillars. Above the deck level, a balcony ran the length of the front, probably belonging to the master bedroom.

She could hear voices, low and lazy as they approached the deck. The pool was rectangular and hotel-sized, but looked sparkling clean. A man and a woman sat in the hot tub. She mentally scanned her notes—Tom and Tracy, she decided. Tom was facing her as they arrived and held up a glass in salute, his face flushed from either the heat of the hot tub or the drink. The redhead across from him kept her back turned and made no move of acknowledgement or interest.

Another woman reclined in a lounger under an umbrella, with a bonnet style hat pulled over her eyes, a paperback lying open-spined and upside down beside her. Jill, thought Abby, protecting her skin from the elements. Probably the only sunbathing she did was au naturel to prevent tan lines. She was the actress whose parts Daddy's money seemed always ready to buy.

There was a lone swimmer in the pool, doing laps as well as possible considering the length of the pool, looping his turns gracefully at each end and showing a practiced switch from a crawl to a backstroke. His hair was dark and his body well-tanned and muscular-looking. Had to be Brady, Bret's oldest. There was no sign of Kara or Nikki, but a heartbeat later, Nikki burst onto the deck in a tornado of energy.

"Abby! You haven't changed a bit!" Nikki came bouncing down the steps to grab her in a hug, then stood back to give her a steady gaze full of meaning, which Abby had no means of interpreting without help. Dressed in blue jeans and a light pink shirt cropped above the waist, she looked like the girl next door. *Just shows how deceiving appearances can be*, thought Abby, her thoughts flying to Neil. How deceiving were his looks?

"Everyone's here." Nikki waved a hand expansively, the sun striking the stones in the large amethyst she wore on her right index finger. "Tom's in the hot tub." Another drinker's salute with a slightly slurred greeting. The flush was definitely from the drink, Abby decided. "Tracy, too." She gestured at the redhead who turned slightly to give a quizzical smile. "Jill's the shy one over there hiding from the evil effects of the sun." Jill moved slightly, which could be interpreted as either an acknowledgment of the greeting or an effort to find a more comfortable position. "Brady's the energetic one in the pool, and Lord knows, as usual, where Kara is. Now I'm going to steal you away to get you settled." She took the suitcase from Neil's grasp and started for the door. Abby obediently trotted after her. Didn't everyone? She cast a smile of thanks over her shoulder at Neil, who was by now looking at the hot tub with a frown. His pleasant face was transformed into a grimace. Was the look meant for Tom or Tracy? Or perhaps for Brady, visible over their heads as he made another turn. Or even the blank space Nikki had occupied until a moment ago?

Nikki ushered her upstairs, shushing her as she opened her mouth to begin asking the obvious questions. "Later," she mouthed. "Your room's at the back," she said. "Sorry it doesn't have an en-suite. The main bathroom is next door." She opened the door to a square room with pale blue walls and a low-pile carpet in a slightly darker shade of the same color. A double bed was covered with a blue and rose duvet and topped with matching pillows. A small dresser and desk stood side by side along the near wall. The window across from the door was tall and marked in small panes. It opened shutter style. Abby was glad to see it was screened and hoped mosquitoes were not omnipresent as they had been at home. She noted the standing fan in the corner as an added cooling option.

Nikki followed her gaze to the fan. "There's no central air. On an island, it's not really necessary and besides, it would be too much of a drain on the generator. You'll find it cools down nicely at night." She peered back down the hallway and closed the door, motioning for Abby to sit beside her on the bed. "I'll explain everything to you, but not here. Let's go for a walk around the other side of the island, where no one will hear."

A walk was not really what Abby wanted after her trek up from the dock. A nap seemed to be more in order, but what the heck? Curiosity wouldn't let her rest until she knew what Nikki was up to her pretty little neck into anyhow. That Nikki was serious and worried was apparent in every jerky move her expressive hands made, with every little jump at real or imagined noises, and by the frown lines that seemed to be settling permanently on her forehead and upper nose.

They walked back down to the deck. Nikki waved at the others. "Taking Abby for the royal tour," she threw over her shoulder at her seemingly unconcerned guests.

They took the pathway in the opposite direction from the dock and followed it down to the shore where it turned right and ran parallel to the edges of the tree line. It was covered in loose gravel that crunched under their footsteps. For a short, tiny person, Nikki had a long stride and Abby struggled to keep up.

"Nikki, what's going on? This has nothing to do with a biography. That's apparent. But I think you need to do some explaining."

Nikki glanced over her shoulder and stopped for a minute to listen. "In a minute. There's a spot a little farther along where we can sit. I'll tell you then."

Abby followed along dutifully. Nikki continued at a fast pace. Very little of the island was open, from what Abby could see. The path ran out of gravel and became a dirt path, worn into the grass just above, where it met the rocky incline to the water. They passed a trail that led down to an old pier, smaller than the one they landed at. On the other side, it ran into the woods but she could see a clearing and made out a log structure.

"What's that,?" she asked, pointing.

"Oh, that's just the old cabin the previous owners built. It's tiny and no good for anything. Bret just never got around to having it torn down. I don't know why they built on this side of the island anyhow. It's much more sheltered on our side with lots more room to build without cutting down a forest first."

Abby thought the uncut forest was probably the reason they had chosen the spot. She struggled to keep pace with Nikki and was relieved when they finally came to a stop. The shoreline jutted farther into the lake at the point with a rocky outcrop leaving a long, natural seat on the stone. Nikki finally settled on the rock. Abby followed suit.

"Now, what's going on?" she asked.

"Abby, someone's trying to kill me."

Chapter Eight

Abby knew her mouth had dropped open, but couldn't seem to get enough control over her muscles to clamp it shut. "You can't be serious!"

"I'm very serious."

"Then the police are the ones you should be talking to, not me."

"Tried that." Nikki reached into her pocket and pulled out a small pack of Rothmans, lighting one with a shaking hand. "I gave these up. But now..."

"What happened? What makes you think someone is trying to kill you? "

Nikki took another drag on her cigarette and dropped it to the ground, rubbing it into the dirt with her toe. "It happened two weeks ago. Everyone was at the house for the weekend. Tom, Brady, Tracy, Jill, Neil, Kara, and me."

"Your dramatis personae."

She gave a weak smile. "We were having a policy weekend; Bret used to have them, sort of a combination family get-together with some business discussions thrown in. I wanted to go over some changes I was planning to make—give everyone a head's up, so to speak."

"Where did the attempt on your life come into this cosy gathering?"

"You never did sarcasm well, Abby. We have a small conservatory at the house that's always been my domain. I paint a little; remember I used to in college?" Abby nodded. She remembered Nikki wasn't half bad, but not serious about art in any way. She was more interested in the art of others, and had majored in Fine Arts. It was just another one of those things she did well. "Well, anyhow," she went on. "I like to relax there when things get a little difficult. I keep my art supplies there. Sunday morning, I took my coffee into the conservatory after breakfast and left to get some shears to trim one of the plants. When I got back, I started to take a drink from my mug..." She stopped and reached for her cigarette pack again.

"Go on, Nikki."

"Just as I was going to take a gulp, the phone rang. I stopped as my mouth touched the coffee and it stung. I realized it wasn't coffee just in time. Someone had replaced it with paint thinner. If I'd taken a big gulp and swallowed before realizing what it was...sort of saved by the bell."

"Is there any way you could have grabbed the wrong mug? Or someone moved it by mistake?"

"No. Someone did it deliberately. And that wasn't the first thing."

"Go on."

"A week earlier, I was driving down the road out to the highway. The house is secluded and the road out is cut into rock face. As I rounded the corner, a huge boulder came hurtling down at the car. As luck happened, I'd just swerved to miss a gopher on the road, but if I hadn't, the rock would have hit me."

"But, Nikki, that sort of thing can happen naturally. You can't be sure that was done by someone deliberately."

"I wasn't. Not until the paint thinner."

"What did the police say?"

"Hysterical woman in a depressive state following personal setbacks, too much imagination."

"They didn't actually say that."

"No, but they might as well have. Abby." She stood up and grabbed her hands between her own, staring earnestly into her eyes. "Abby, I know someone is trying to kill me. And it has to be one of the people here on the island now."

"So what can I possibly do that the police can't?"

"It's not can't so much as won't. They don't think I'm in

any danger."

"Nikki, if this is true..."

"It is, I swear."

"If it's true, I don't see how I can help. You'd be better off with a bodyguard, or a private detective."

"I can't have a bodyguard forever. I have to find out who it is so I can get on with my life. As for the private detective, I did hire someone to find out if there was anything about my nearest and dearest I should know but didn't. That's where the dossiers came from. I left them in your dresser drawer. Nighttime reading. You may be tested." She gave a weak smile.

She was missing something. "Nikki, you've left someone out."

"Who?"

"Your husband."

"No, it can't have anything to do with Daniel. He was in Vancouver that weekend. One of our managers quit suddenly and he had to troubleshoot. Besides, he's the only one without a motive."

"How so?"

"Bret and I had our wills made at the same time. He left everything to me, and if I outlived him, my will passed the holdings on equally between Brady, Jill, and Kara."

"That seems a little odd."

"Bret knew Kara wasn't able to manage her finances if anything happened to him, and he wasn't too sure about Brady or Jill." She sighed. "It was a funny situation really. Bret loved his kids and would do anything for them. He was very generous financially, but they were never able to prove themselves to him as being capable. He felt more confident in me, I guess."

"So what about Daniel?"

"I told you, Daniel has nothing to do with this."

"Humor me."

"We made up an agreement when we married. Daniel runs the show at Charms as long as we're married and he has all he can spend. If I die, the estate goes to the kids." Her glance shifted away across the water and Abby knew she was leaving out something. "He'd have no reason to want me dead. And anyhow, I told you, he was out of town that weekend."

"How about the day of the boulder?"

"Well, he was there then, but then so was everyone else."

"Another family conflab?"

"Yes."

"I still don't know what you think I can do. Surely you know these people better than I do. They're your family."

"That's the trouble. I'm too close. No objectivity, you see. Abby, you were always the one who could ferret out the truth when people try to hide things. Please do this for me. If I don't find out soon, I'll become the hysterical woman the police think I am."

"Finding out who has murder in their agenda is a little different from finding out who put the graffiti on the canteen wall or who stole all of Jessica's bras." She sat down again, pulling Nikki with her. "Tell me more about these changes you were planning to make. I assume that's where the possible motives come in?"

She nodded. "I'm going to sell off a lot of the Cummings holdings. I'm not really up to Bret's caliber in running businesses. I want to liquidate most of the holdings and invest them in something a little more secure. The kids' inheritances will be safe and I'll be able to make a life for myself. I'll keep Charms, of course. That's all mine."

"But surely, you have people to run the various holdings. You don't need to be personally involved."

"With Bret gone, I don't know who I can rely on any more. I'd rather just get out from under. And we went through a few difficulties the last couple of years. Bret had the savvy to weather that, but I don't think I do, and in these economic times..."

"So how does that affect everyone?"

"Well, Tom's not too thrilled. But he has his own company as well as working in ours. I don't know why he's so upset. He should be nearly ready to retire anyhow; he's two years older than Bret. He's sixty-two. Neil's so close-mouthed you never know what he's thinking. He had his own law practice before he worked for us. I suppose he could do that again, but he's used to the easy money he gets with the company. Brady and Tracy both work for the real estate firm, so I guess they don't like the thought of looking for new jobs. And Jill—well, all she wants is someone to take her seriously as an actress. I think it's a little late for that. Really, I don't see what everyone was making such a fuss about. I'm looking after everyone's interests."

"And Kara?"

Nikki shifted her gaze to the lake again. "Kara's had a few problems, and we don't see eye to eye on much of anything these days, but that's just teenage angst. She's my daughter, Abby. She couldn't be responsible."

Abby thought Kara couldn't be ruled out that easily. Putting something in a coffee mug sounded like a teenage prank carried too far more than an action that could be attributed to business executives or corporate lawyers. Ouch! Why did Abby experience a twinge at that thought? During her brief encounter with Neil, she'd felt a connection to him. *So much for being objective, Abby. Pull your socks up; you have to consider everybody.* She let out a long breath. That last thought meant she was actually considering Nikki's proposal to ferret out a murderer. But how could she not at least try? It looked as if Nikki was running out of options. That was if there was an actual plot. Abby didn't rule out the police conclusion of hysteria. It had been a difficult year for the family, but that meant pressure on all its members, not just Nikki. Maybe someone did feel pushed over the edge.

"Do you really think coming to a remote island with a handful of people, including a possible murderer, was the thing to do? Wouldn't you be safer at home with a good security system?"

"And hide from my family for the rest of my life? I don't think that's an option. I need to know. Abby, it's up to you now."

"What if something happens and we need to make contact with the outside world? You don't have a phone on the island."

"No land line, but there's sporadic cell phone service. You can't connect at the main house, something to do with the rocky terrain in the center of the island, but if you walk down to the end,"—she pointed ahead—"you can usually get service. Did you bring your cell? I didn't. I know Kara has hers. I think that's why she disappears all the time; she heads around the island to the point so she can text her friends. Then if you really need to contact someone, there are the boats. Bronco keeps them in top condition. He always comes a day earlier and gets everything set up for us. I guess I shouldn't complain so much about him. He's really an asset in many ways."

Abby's mind was still on Kara. If she was a typical teen-ager, Abby felt there were probably more reasons to disap-pear than texting. "Doesn't Kara have plans for the summer? Job? Camp? Is she going back to school in the fall?"

Nikki sighed. "She's going through a bad phase. Bret's death hit her hard. She was Daddy's little girl, but even be-fore then we'd had problems. She got into a weird crowd of kids, Abby, and got hooked on some bad stuff. We put her into rehab and it seemed to do the trick. We switched schools and she was doing well. Then the plane crash...well, it threw the whole family into a vortex. Kara took it hardest of all. I'm afraid she might slip back into her old patterns, and I need to have her where I can keep an eye on her."

"She's seventeen, Nikki. You can't watch her forever."

"I know, but just until summer's over, I want her near me. I know she doesn't feel the same about it. That's why she's never at the house. I think she hates me. I know she's not forgiven me for marrying Daniel."

Abby bit her tongue. It wasn't going to help if she told Nikki she agreed with Kara about the hasty remarriage being a foolish move.

"Back to Daniel..."

"What?" The reply came out as an explosive. Obviously Nikki didn't want him under consideration, but was it because she knew he had nothing to do with all this, or because she didn't want to examine her own feelings too deeply?

"He's not here this week either?"

"No." Short answers were becoming the norm here.

"Why?"

"Same problem as before. He's in Vancouver sorting out new management. The new one he hired before didn't work out so it's back to square one." Nikki stood up suddenly and threw her second cigarette into the dirt. "Let's get back. I've told everyone you're doing Bret's biography and asked them to answer any questions you have. That should give you a chance to size everyone up. Those files are in your top draw-er. We'll get better acquainted over dinner. Hopefully, Kara will show up."

"Before we go, what about staff? You said in your phone call you had a couple here."

"Bronco and Irene. They're a married couple. Been with us for years. Bret met Bronco at some mining camp and brought him and Irene back to work for us. Irene is a great cook, moderately good housekeeper, and Bronco does a little bit of everything. I have files on them too, as much as I know. The detective traced Bronco back to a few shady dealings. I asked Bret to fire him once, but he wouldn't hear of it."

"Why?"

Nikki correctly assumed the question was for the first part of the sentence. "I overheard a conversation between him and Irene. Apparently, he was into drugs once and I didn't want him in the house with Kara."

"What did Bret say?"

"He said it was old history."

"But after Bret died? You could have let him go."

"Laziness, I guess. Or maybe because Irene is such a good employee, he's the bad with the good. I've kept an eye on him, and Kara never goes near him. I think she hates him more than me for some reason, so he seemed safe."

The walk back was a quiet one. Abby tried to picture the people she had met so far in the role of murderer without success. Maybe the private detective's information would give her some insight into them. Nikki didn't say a word. Abby's heart went out to her. Whether it was true or not, it must be a horrible feeling to think that someone close to you actually wanted you dead.

Chapter Nine

When they got back to the house, Nikki went into the lounge. "I could do with a drink," she said tonelessly.

Abby headed for the stairs, pausing in the doorway as she passed the kitchen. A short, powerful-looking woman of about forty stood by the kitchen island dressed in denim shorts and t-shirt, covered by an old-fashioned apron. She was rolling dough with a strong rhythm that made her dark brown ponytail bounce. Irene. Abby swirled around as she felt a hot breath on the back of her neck. "Need something, Mrs. Addison?" She'd not heard his footsteps on the tile hallway, even in the quiet of the afternoon.

"Just getting oriented." She forced herself to smile. "You're Bronco?"

He returned her smile coolly and nodded, pushing past her into the kitchen as if she were of no consequence. He made no effort to avoid touching her. The contact left her chilled. Before she turned to the staircase, she watched Bronco sit down at the kitchen table, and Irene interrupted her pastry making to fetch him a cup of coffee. Not a word was exchanged between them. A couple on the outs? Or maybe they were just so accustomed to each other they didn't need words. She wished she could see their facial expressions, but both were turned away.

Upstairs, she pulled the file folder out of the top dresser

drawer and began to read. Her basic information on Tom seemed to match the detective's, but he added a few questions about Tom's solvency in his own firm, with the addition that the revenue service was interested in auditing his affairs. Abby couldn't see how Nikki's death would benefit him in any way; according to Nikki, he wasn't in her will. But if he was in financial trouble, the sale of Bret's holdings would cut into his income. He needed a good income with two ex-wives and three children between them. Abby noted the extended family get-togethers didn't stretch to include the cousins.

She scanned the information on Brady and Tracy. According to the detective, Mike Jergens, their marriage was in deep trouble. Brady had had numerous affairs and was becoming less discreet with each one. Tracy wanted a child. She had visited various fertility clinics in the hope of becoming pregnant with no success. Did she blame Brady, or was it just that he wasn't as interested in producing an heir as she was? Nikki's death would certainly give Brady a financial windfall, but Tracy? As long as she was married to Brady, she'd benefit. On second thought, that would give her a motive. If Nikki died, Tracy's divorce settlement, if her marriage went that way, would certainly be larger. Brady didn't appear to have any money of his own, so a divorce now would leave her practically penniless.

Jill seemed to be straightforward. She'd always wanted to be an actress and Bret had always fostered that interest. Jergens' file didn't say if she was any good or not, but if she needed constant infusions of investment to get her parts, she mustn't be as good as she thought she was. Nikki's death would certainly benefit her—she'd get her share of Bret's fortune.

There was no file on Kara. Nikki must have balked at the idea of investigating her own daughter. Either that or she had included her but kept it to herself. There couldn't be much about a seventeen-year-old girl her mother didn't know. Then she thought back to Mandy's teen years and revised her opinion. Maybe there was very little about a seventeen-year-old her mother *does* know. In any case, Nikki didn't consider her to be the threat, but how else would a mother feel? Abby reserved judgment on Kara; she hadn't even met her yet.

She slid out the file on Bronco and felt the hair stand on the back of her neck. She had a bad feeling about him and didn't see how Nikki felt comfortable with him around, no matter how good a worker Irene was. Bronco was born William Federstone, but had earned the nickname Bronco when he did the rodeo circuit as a young man. It stuck with him. He gravitated to the oilfields, and while there, picked up a drug habit. He was caught in a random drug test and fired. After that, he worked his way around the country, married Irene, and they became a team, working as a couple at remote logging and mining camps. This is where Bret met him. Something must have intrigued Bret about him and he hired him after supervising his stay at a rehab center. His job with Bret was dependent on his staying clean and sober, and they had an agreement that he take regular drug tests. After a few years, Bret apparently gained enough confidence in Bronco to move him and his wife into their household staff and they'd been there ever since. Irene's background was simple. After graduating high school, she'd worked as a cook in northern mines until she met Bronco. They had no children. What did she see in Bronco? Who knew, but some women seemed to prefer men who traveled with a hint of danger.

Abby realized she'd kept Neil's file till last. Accident or design? She opened it and began reading. Most of it she knew—his law career in his father's firm cut short when they had a big blow-up over a case. He had moved from there to a private practice, but it didn't really thrive. Neither did his marriage; apparently, his wife couldn't stand the lifestyle change and left him for another lawyer in his father's firm. The question arose as to whether they'd been an item before Neil split with his father, but it didn't seem pertinent here. They had no children, although she gave birth just nine months after she left him for Trevor. If either one of them brought up the question of the baby's paternity, there was no note of it. His mother died of cancer. Until then he had kept in touch with her even though his estrangement with his father never ended. His father was still alive, retired, but not remarried. Neil and Bret met through some contract work Neil had done and they became friends. Shortly after, Bret made him an offer and he closed his business to be on Bret's payroll. His income was solid, but his expenses were higher. He was apparently a collector. Mostly, he was interested in pre-historic artifacts and made a habit of attending auctions, spending more than he could afford. That, according to Jergens, seemed to be his only vice, but if he were teetering on the brink of insolvency, losing his position with Cummings would put his collector's prizes in jeopardy. Abby had met a collector once before and knew the passion they extended to their possessions. Neil wouldn't part with his pieces easily, but could it be a motive for murder? What would he gain by Nikki's death? The company would still possibly be liquidated, but maybe he had some leverage with Brady and Jill, who would make the decisions then.

Abby sighed and replaced the folder in the drawer. Time to go down to dinner and meet everyone officially. She traded her shorts for a pair of white slacks and her tee for a short-sleeved pale blue shirt. She swapped her sneakers for sandals. They were a bit scruffy, but would have to do.

As she entered the lounge, everyone was there, drinks in hand. Tom waved a hand in her direction, pointing toward the drinks cabinet, and Nikki, looking more subdued than usual, told her to help herself. Neil was already at the drink stand and asked her preference.

"No liquor, please. Just a glass of red wine, if there's some open."

"There'll be some on the table for dinner," he said, looking around and not seeing any wine. "How about a glass of sherry for now?"

She took a small glass of the pale amber drink from him and sipped. She wasn't really that fond of sherry, but it would do. At least it wasn't sweet. She had to keep her head clear, so no double rums tonight.

She scanned the room. Kara sat in a far corner, head bent over an iPad, totally ignoring the rest of the assembly. Her dark hair—must be dyed, both Bret and Nikki were fair—was streaked with magenta and half covered her face. What she could see was heavily made up, with kohl rings around her eyes and bright red lip color making a gash in her pale-painted skin.

Jill sat deeply entrenched in a comfortable chair, slouched in a manner not conducive to an actress's posture. She looked very put together in white capris and a silk lilac blouse. Brady and Tracy sat on couches on opposite sides of the room. From the lack of any sort of eye contact, no one would think they were a couple. Tom was leaning ahead on the edge of another comfortable chair, close to the drink table, Abby noted.

Neil motioned her to join him on a padded bench at a right angle to the fireplace and facing Nikki, who sat, feet curled up under her on a similar bench. Conversation was sporadic, Tom's voice a little loud, Kara in her own world, Jill concentrating on a snag on one of her nails. Nikki participated like an automaton. Neil seemed to take the conversational lead, but it was hard-going. It was a relief when Irene poked her head around the corner to announce dinner.

They managed to keep the conversation steady and civilized through the cold berry soup and the entree—pickerel with little roasted potatoes, regular and sweet, sided by tiny peas and glazed carrots. Irene cleared the plates and brought in coffee to go with the pie Abby had seen her making that afternoon. Tom opened another bottle of wine.

Nikki pushed her plate away. "Tomorrow morning, I want us all to have a meeting at eleven o'clock to take care of some business," she said. "Neil, you have everything I asked you to prepare?" He nodded. "We've got some decisions to make about where the company's going."

"Don't you mean you have decisions to make?" asked Jill.

"If that's how you'd like to put it."

Tom set down his glass. "How come the boy wonder isn't joining us?"

"I told you before. Daniel has business to take care of in Vancouver."

"It's none of his business anyhow," said Brady. "He's not family."

"Hear, hear," mumbled Tracy in a rare show of marital accord.

Just your typical happy family, thought Abby, becoming aware that more than one family member was looking at her questioningly. Nikki chose that moment to change the topic.

"You've all met Abby," she said, "but I didn't tell you why she was here. I've decided to do a biography of Bret, and Abby's going to write it for me. I hope you'll all cooperate with her. I know she'll be picking your brains for juicy tidbits." The reaction was mixed. Tom let out a roar of laughter, Neil looked at her speculatively like a specimen under a microscope, Jill and Tracy looked bored, Brady incredulous. Kara excused herself and went out to the deck. Abby watched their faces in turn, but saw mostly amusement, certainly not fear or suspicion. She felt a little deflated, as though she had been quite nicely put in her place. After coffee, the others adjourned to the lounge. Abby decided to make her first set of inquiries and went outside to find Kara.

She sat down beside Kara on the deck stairs, one step below her, holding her wineglass against her warm face. Kara didn't look up. Abby knew she wouldn't, but seated below her, she had the advantage of viewpoint.

"You don't appear very enthused about the idea of my writing a book about your father."

"Whatever." She continued to play her game.

"Not enjoying your summer, are you?"

She got her attention with that. An underappreciated teenager usually took advantage of a chance to vent, especially if there was a chance it would get back to her mother.

"Nikki's being a bitch."

Abby wondered when the Mother had ended and the Nikki began—probably at the onset of puberty. Thank heavens Mandy had never felt the need to address her by her first name.

"How so?"

"Emma's in Europe backpacking." She began to tick her friends off on her fingers. "Sammy and Ash are working the summer at a camp in the Rockies and having tons of fun. Even Eden's got a great summer job. And where's Kara?" She gestured theatrically—the sense of drama seemed to run in the family. "Stuck on an island with no TV, practically no cell service, and no friends. Because my stupid mother won't trust me."

"Given her a lot of reason to do that, have you?" She risked the comment, flavoring it with a smile to take the edge off the sarcasm. It did the job.

Kara seemed tickled by the response and dimpled into a smile. The girl was really attractive, Abby thought, if only she'd do something with herself and lose the sulky Goth look.

"I'm a teenager," she said. "Bugging your parents is part of the job description." Then her face clouded. "Oh, I suppose you heard about the rehab thing. That's old news. I don't do anything now except the odd bit of booze I can sneak." She looked at Abby's wine glass. "I don't suppose..,"

"No," said Abby firmly.

"Oh well." Kara didn't seem upset. "Worth a try." She made a face. "If she's worried about trust, she should be looking at that creep she married."

"You don't like Daniel?"

"He's a dirt-bag. Keeps ogling me and I'm his step-daughter. He cops a feel with Jill and Tracy whenever he thinks he can get away with it. Slime ball," she ended with a sneer.

"Don't they say anything to Nikki?"

"Naw. They know which side their bread is buttered on. Nikki gets to make all the money decisions. Jill wants to hit her up for backing for another play and Tracy's always looking at another fertility clinic. They're expensive. I don't know why anybody'd go to all that trouble just to have a kid." She went back to her game. The conversation was over as far as Kara was concerned.

Abby slipped down the walk toward the edge of the lake, following the path she and Nikki had taken earlier. She stood and watched the water in its gentle slapping of the pebbled shore, wondering what she'd gotten herself into. Nikki had gone over supper from forced bonhomie to a lethargy that was very out of character. Was someone really trying to kill her? Or had the chaos that had marred her life for the past year caused a personality meltdown. Then she remembered the firmness with which Nikki had announced the morning's meeting. She wasn't the type to give in easily. Too bad Abby wouldn't be part of that meeting; she'd learn a lot.

She turned and did a recon of the rest of the grounds. She could see Bronco behind the house spraying something on some bushes. Weed killer? She thought of Nikki's paint thinner and shuddered. She deliberately went the opposite direction. Her short meeting with Bronco was enough to last her for now, but tomorrow, she'd have to gird her loins—she giggled at the picture that phrase invoked and thought, *Wrong sex. Is Nikki's hysteria rubbing off?*—and find a way to talk to him, preferably in sight of the others.

As she crossed the yard behind the generator shed, she could hear a murmur of conversation. She stopped around the corner and could make out the lowered voices. "You've got to talk to her." It was Tom's voice and surprisingly lucid. He had given all the signs of overdrinking earlier. He certainly sobered up quickly; either that or he'd been putting on a show with an agenda of his own.

"She's your sister-in-law. It would sound better coming

from you." Neil. Abby strained to hear the words and, at the same time, looked for her best exit. She needed to rehearse what she would say if caught eavesdropping.

"She hasn't listened to a word I've said since Bret died. If she had, do you think she'd be married to that gigolo?"

"We'll have to put up a united front at the meeting. But she has the final say in everything. Damn Bret! Why did he have to leave her with all the power? I knew the will was going to cause problems, but I didn't think it would be so soon."

"You're the one that drew them up."

"And how was I to know the plane would go down in the wilderness? Unless you had a premonition."

"I loved Bret. We didn't always see eye to eye, but brothers never do. If you think I could have had anything to do with that crash..." He switched gears. "You have as much to lose as I do."

"Yes, but not as much to gain."

"What do you mean by that?" Abby heard a rustle in the tree behind her. Squirrel, she thought, but the conversation stopped and she knew they had heard it too. She backed up a few steps beyond the shed and made more noise than usual reapproaching the shed. She stopped in feigned surprise. "Oh, hi," she said to the two now silent men. "Just getting my bearings. Beautiful night, isn't it?"

Tom just glowered and walked toward the house. Neil gave her a piercing look that suggested he knew exactly when she had arrived and how much she heard. *Tricks of a lawyer*, she thought. *Always make them think you know everything.* Then Neil smiled and took her arm. "I'll give you the guided tour," he said. "Although, there's not much to see. Just storage sheds. The generator's in there." He pointed at the building she'd been hiding behind. They walked around the point together and made their way back to the house. Neil's verbosity on the plane had escaped him. She wondered what he was thinking. He was obviously privy to all the secrets of the family. He would have drawn up Nikki's will as well as Bret's. The conversation between Tom and Neil had suggested a collusion of sorts. What could they be planning that would benefit them both? Neil's persuasive powers must have been absent when Bret laid out the terms of his will. Neil went along with Bret even though he disagreed with the idea. But then, he was a payroll attorney, not a private consulting one. He would do as he was told.

No one seemed in a mood to talk when she got back. Kara had disappeared again, also Tom. Neither Jill nor Tracy seemed inclined to conversation and Brady was back in the pool. She heard Nikki in the kitchen talking over tomorrow's menu with Irene and paused in the doorway. Nikki came out to walk her up the stairs.

"I noticed the bedroom doors don't have locks," Abby said.

"Now why would anyone want to lock out their nearest and dearest?" That was the second time she'd heard Nikki use that phrase, and it was even more acidic this time.

"Don't you think you should be locking yours?"

"I've been pulling my dresser against the door at night," Nikki admitted. "But I think I'm rather safe at night."

"How so?"

"Well, the rock thing and the paint thinner were both aimed at making it look like an accident, so I don't think anyone is going to smother me or shoot me in my sleep."

"Reassuring." She paused at her bedroom door. "Be careful, Nikki."

"That's what I'm trying to do."

"I don't think your morning meeting comes under that heading."

"Business is business," she replied tersely, and turned toward her room.

Abby changed into her pajamas, then pulled on her robe to visit the bathroom next door. There was no other sign of activity upstairs. She hoped Nikki was secure in her room. After she'd flossed and brushed, she decided to have another look at the folder Nikki had left her. Maybe now that she'd talked to everyone, however briefly, something would leap out at her. She opened the folder and stared at the top file. Abby knew she had looked at Neil's file last and left it on top. Now the top one was the report on Bronco. Someone had been in her room and read the files. She thought back over the evening. Anyone could have slipped into her room while she was out on the grounds. She looked at the dresser and started to tug it across the room. Nikki wasn't the only one who needed to barricade herself in for the night.

Chapter
Ten

Abby woke suddenly in the morning with the light slash-
ing across her bed from the east-facing window. She was
surprised that she had slept through the night, given her
emotional turmoil of yesterday. She didn't have the choice of
closing her eyes for a lie-in; the pressure on her bladder was
tremendous. "No more wine before bed," she said out loud,
her voice croaky with sleep. Dragging a heavy piece of furniture across the room with a bursting bladder was not the
easiest of tasks, but she pulled the dresser aside far enough
to make her exit and dashed for the bathroom.

No one appeared to be standing in line for this bathroom
and she knew there were two more in the house, so Abby
took her time with a hot shower, trying to wash away her
negative thoughts. By the time she toweled off, she had almost convinced herself Nikki was imagining the danger. The
paint thinner sounded more and more like a prank gone
wrong or an accident. And the boulder? It must be pretty difficult to make a rogue boulder roll exactly where and when
you wanted it. Surely if someone were trying to eliminate
Nikki, they would find a more certain way to arrange it. Then
she remembered the displaced folders in her desk and shivered. She slipped back into her room and changed into jeans
and a peach-colored shirt. A quick swipe at her hair with a
brush and some moisturizer and eye liner and she was ready

to face the day.

Downstairs, she grabbed some toast from the warming tray on the sideboard—just like an old English manor, she thought—and poured a coffee. No one else was around, so she took her coffee and toast out to the deck. There was a swimmer in the pool doing laps. Tracy, Abby deduced from the uncapped auburn hair. Jill was doing a Salute to the Sun on a yoga mat with a totally absorbed expression. It must take a bit of work to keep up the actress figure, thought Abby, glad at the moment to be a somewhat frowsy near-fifty. It took a lot of pressure off, not being a sex object. In other situations, she sometimes felt differently, but at the moment, wasn't slightly envious. She wondered about Jill's love life. No mention had been made of a man, past or present, in her life.

Jill finished her routine, folded her mat, and came to sit beside Abby. She picked up a glass of water and drank deeply. No wrinkle-inducing coffee for her.

"Tell me about yourself, Jill," she said, believing Bret's biography ruse should give her carte blanche to ask questions of everyone. "Nikki told me you were an actress, but nothing about the kind of work you do. Are you mainly interested in the stage, or have you done television? Do you have something planned now?"

Jill's face was truly lovely when animated by a smile. Her dark brown hair was short but thick with a bit of natural wave. Unlike Brady, who had easily-tanned skin, she had inherited her father's fair complexion, which made a perfect setting for the dark hair and blue eyes. Abby wondered about their mother; she must have been the one who had passed on the dark hair shared by Brady and Jill. Pictures of her were noticeably absent in the family archives. She only knew she had died young, before Bret made his fortune and became interesting fodder for the gossip pages. The two children were still young when Bret had married Nikki, but Kara was quite a bit younger than Bret's children from his first marriage.

"I have a project in the works," said Jill. "A good friend of mine has the rights to a marvelous play, and we're trying to get backing for it. The lead role is the best I've been offered yet." The smile faded a little. "I know Dad would have jumped at the chance to back it; it's a sure-fire success, one of those chances that only comes along once in a lifetime.

Nikki's being a little difficult about it, though." She bright-
ened again. "I'm sure I'll be able to convince her."

"It must have been a bit of a shock, having your father
leave Nikki in charge of everything instead of passing it on
directly to his children."

"Oh, we knew the terms of the will," Jill said. "We just
never thought it would come up so soon. Dad was in such
good health. He should have left those trips to someone on
his staff, but he did like adventure. I think he had more fun
checking out new projects than he did in the boardroom.
That's how he relaxed."

"Did they ever determine the cause of the accident?"

"Oh, yes, they had a hearing. It was a combination of
things, bad weather, loss of visibility, and lack of experience
on the part of the pilot."

"I thought Bret would have made sure of the experience
of his pilots."

"Oh, he did, but at the last minute, his regular pilot got
sick and this fellow was a replacement. I think he was new to
the area. There was some talk about inconsistencies in the
flight plan he filed."

"I'm sorry, Jill," Abby said sincerely. It was always sad to
see a life cut short, especially such a robust one as Bret's.

"We all miss him tremendously." Then Jill's face darkened. "Well, most of us anyhow."

Guessing she referred to Nikki, Abby said, "I'm sure Nikki
was quite lost without him, but it must have been hard on
the family to see her remarry so soon."

"It's just that Daniel is so different from Dad. Well, no,
it's more than that, but she could have shown a little more
discernment in her choice. He's a bit of a creep."

"How so?"

"If I were Nikki, I'd be wondering about some of his out
of town trips and just how necessary they are. A man like
Daniel should be kept on a short leash." From Jill's darkened
expression, Abby interpreted that to include the ultimate,
"and possibly be put down." If it had been Daniel whose life
had been under threat, she would have been spoiled for
choice in picking suspects.

Jill stood, and grabbed her glass and mat. "Nice talking to
you." She disappeared into the house.

Abby finished her toast and set the plate down on the side

table. She wondered about the wisdom of a second cup of coffee, but figured she should give her plumbing a rest after last night. She should take up Jill's habits and drink water instead.

Tracy crawled out of the pool and wrapped herself in a large blue terry towel. She blotted some of the moisture out of her hair and pulled it into a semblance of neatness with her hands. Even with no makeup and damp from the pool, she was beautiful. It was difficult to understand Brady's fascination with other women.

She smiled at Abby on the way past. "Any coffee left? I think I'll join you. I love the mornings out here." It was the first time since she'd arrived she'd heard anyone other than Nikki say something positive about the island. Come to think of it, it was also the first time Tracy had spoken to her. Things were looking up. When Tracy sat back down on the steps, she wasted no time giving a reason.

"Why are you really here?"

"Weren't you there when Nikki told everyone about Bret's biography?"

"I didn't believe that for a moment. I can see Jill wanting one done, but Nikki—she's always been too caught up in the present to be reminiscing. Besides, I'm sure she'd do it herself. Why are you really here? Is it something to do with Bret's accident?"

"Why would you think that? As far as I know, Bret's accident was ruled to be just that, an accident."

"Tom thought you might be acting for a private investigator's firm. He always wondered about it. He said it was strange that pilot getting sick all of a sudden. He disappeared after the accident. Did you know that?"

"No, I didn't, but that's not why I'm here." It could be why Tom showed signs of dual personality, though. Maybe he had his suspicions about Bret's death and thought if he played the drunk card, people would let things slip. But who or what did he suspect? And why did Tracy seem to be privy to his ideas? Of course, Tom was Brady's uncle, not hers, and age gaps rarely stood in the way of romance. She remembered from dinner that although Tracy and Tom sat opposite each other, they avoided eye contact. She thought at the time it was indifference, but maybe it was more in the line of posturing.

"I do write biographies, Tracy," she said, and taking the

plunge, decided to be honest. "You're right, though. That's not why I'm here." She stopped Tracy in her self-congratulatory smile. "It's not about Bret, though. It's about Nikki."

"Nikki?"

"She's had a couple of close calls recently, and she wonders if someone might be behind them."

"That's ridiculous."

"Why is it more ridiculous than to think there was something suspicious in Bret's death?"

"If someone is trying to do away with Nikki, they're not very good at it."

"They might get better with practice," said Abby grimly. "Tracy, you were there when Nikki nearly drank that paint thinner. What's your take on it?"

"Nikki's not the brightest star in the morning." She wrinkled her nose in righteous condemnation of laziness. "I bet she's not even out of bed yet. She was just half asleep and grabbed the wrong mug. She keeps her paint supplies in there. I don't think that thinner would have killed her anyway, probably just given her a bad tummy ache. Is it that toxic?"

"Could be if she took a big enough swallow." Abby chided herself for not doing some research. "What about the rock that nearly hit her car the week before? Do you remember who was at the house that weekend?"

"We all were. But stones are always falling down that cliff. I've had to swerve more than once to avoid a rock."

"All being everybody here now?"

"Yes, plus Daniel. He was at home then. Now, if you're looking for someone wanting to hurt Nikki, there's your best choice."

"But Daniel wasn't there the weekend of the paint thinner."

"No," she said reluctantly. It was obvious she wasn't a member of Daniel's fan club. But then, no one here seemed to be. "Besides, Daniel wouldn't have anything to gain," Tracy went on. "Brady, Jill, and Kara are the ones in Nikki's will. Daniel doesn't get anything."

"Is that what she told you?"

"It isn't true?"

"I haven't seen the will." Abby thought she'd already shared more information than she should, but wanted to stay as close to the truth as possible. "But I would think she'd have made some provision for her husband."

"If she did, she didn't tell Daniel. I've heard him say he gets nothing. But you're right. I bet he is provided for. She probably left him Charms." Abby shot her a quick look, surprised by her perceptiveness.

"Listen," Tracy went on. "If you and I are thinking that way, guaranteed Daniel is too. He's probably found a way to check. Nikki's just fooling herself if she thinks otherwise."

Tom strolled out from the house just then and with a nod at them both, headed for the trail. "Going to take advantage of the day and go for a walk," he said. "See if I can get cell phone connection at the other end."

Tracy lost interest in their conversation and jumped up. "Got to shower and change," she said, "before my hair goes all weird from the chlorine."

Now why did Abby think that in about ten minutes she'd be out for a stroll along the trail? She wondered if Brady guessed, or cared. She'd seen no animosity between him and his uncle if, in fact, he had sensed their mutual attraction. It seemed vaguely incestuous at first glance, but there was no blood relationship between Tracy and Tom, so apart from the moral issue of infidelity, no reason they couldn't get together. What a strange marriage. Brady rarely glanced at his wife when they were together; she'd not even seen them in conversation.

But then were there any marriages that weren't strange in some way? Look at her marriage with Richard. In some ways, it had been perfect. Richard was caring, funny, a great father, loved his home life. Trouble was, he loved life away from home too. The first affair she had caught him out in was shortly after Mandy was born. He swore it would never happen again and she blamed herself a little. Post-partum depression or whatever had left her in a bit of a fugue for months where the only thing that seemed to matter was getting one foot in front of the other for another day. When the fugue lifted, she noticed the change in Richard. He was behaving differently, but not in the way she thought a cheating husband would act. He wasn't remote or distant. In fact, he was over-solicitous, if anything. When she accidently encountered the evidence that he was seeing another agent that worked in his real estate firm and confronted him, he was quick to admit his fault. He only blamed himself, not her.

How could she not forgive him? Besides, she had two young children she couldn't bear to think about raising in a broken home. So, things went on for years. Once or twice she had suspicions, but preferred to ignore them. In every way but that, Richard was nearly perfect. She decided the problem was that Richard loved women. Oh, it wasn't just sex, she knew. Richard actually liked women. He enjoyed their company; he didn't indulge in misogynist jokes. He had this old-fashioned courtesy that made him irresistible, because women realized he liked them. It was a breeding ground for disaster, no matter how good his intentions.

By the time she realized she couldn't ignore his affairs any longer and still maintain a semblance of dignity, Matthew was in Nursing Training and Mandy was a teenager. She asked Richard for a divorce. When she considered the stories she'd heard about friends' divorces, she was amazed about the simplicity of it. She thought back and was sure she and Richard hardly even raised their voices in deciding how best to break up an over twenty year marriage.

Neither of the children seemed to think they were forced into taking sides and managed to share their time with equality and lack of guilt. She'd had a friend once who actually counted the hours her grown daughter spent with her and with her ex and used the tally for leverage in family fights. Luckily, she and Richard were still friends of a sort— well, at least they were civil to each other when they met, maybe friends was stretching it a bit.

She had a funny feeling Mandy still thought there was hope for a reunion between them, but was smart enough not to be caught plotting. Matthew was away from home so much there was no one to plot with.

At the thought of Matthew, she felt that usual tug at the pit of her stomach. She wished he wasn't so far away. She wished he was in a safer place. She wished...well, there was no sense wishing. Danger lurked everywhere in life, not just in remote countries in the midst of genocide, disease, and famine.

He'd be home soon on a visit. He'd timed it to coincide with his birthday, so they'd have a big bash. She wasn't really sure how that was going to work out. Richard's newest interest she found a bit pushy. She constantly inserted herself into any family discussions and even called Abby occasionally. She found it disconcerting, especially as she couldn't really convince herself to like Kelly. She'd so much prefer to have a quiet dinner celebration with Matthew, but Kelly was bound to have Big Plans. She capitalized the term in her thoughts because that's how she saw Kelly, always living in capital letters. *Meow, Abby, will you ever find one of Richard's women suitable?*

"Penny for them." Neil sat down beside her and she felt that familiar rush as his arm brushed her thigh.

"Not worth the going price," she said, now firmly back in the present.

"Can we go for a walk? I'd like to talk to you."

The questioner was about to be questioned, she thought, but set her coffee cup down and willingly agreed.

They walked in silence until they came to the trail down to the boathouse. Had he been watching Tom and deliberately decided to go the other way? She stumbled once on the path and he caught her to steady her. "Flip-flops aren't the best trail walkers," he said.

"If I'd known I was going to be trail walking, I'd have worn my Nikes."

He sat down on the pier and motioned for her to sit beside him.

"Now" he said, "why are you really here?" Second time in an hour she'd been asked that question. She knew there was no sense in continuing the ruse; what one person knew on this island, everyone would know shortly. But Tracy thought she was here to ask about Bret. She'd like to know why Neil thought she was here.

"Nikki wants some help with a biography of Bret."

"Sounds simple, but not plausible."

"Why not?"

"Nikki isn't the type to be concerned about posterity. And I called someone last night to do some checking for me. You're a writer all right, but you write in the field of education. Nikki wouldn't fall into your sphere." She hadn't seen Neil slip out of the house to find an area where he could make a call, which just showed how difficult it would be to track everyone's movements.

"We're old friends. I could make an exception." She paused for bit. "Why do you think she asked me here then?"

"That's what I'm trying to find out." Unlike Tracy, he

wasn't going to give her clues as to what he thought. *That's what you get for talking to lawyers, Abby.*

"I just talked to Tracy. She thinks I'm here to investigate Bret's death." She waited for his reaction, but was disappointed.

"Are you?"

She sighed in defeat. "No." Might as well be open; Neil wasn't going to give anything away. "Nikki is concerned about a couple of close calls she had recently."

Neil let out a whoop of a laugh. "You're here to protect Nikki! Why on earth would anyone want to hurt her?"

"I seem to be uncovering a few reasons. It's not that far-fetched. For instance, the consensus seems to be that she's selling off the holdings. That's what this morning's meeting is all about, right?" He nodded grimly. "Well, that would put Tom, Brady, and Tracy out of a job—and you," she added.

"Losing a job isn't reason to want to put someone out of the way."

"It is if that job has become a real cash cow and the alternatives don't look so bright. Then there's Bret's will leaving Nikki in command. It would be easier for nearly everyone if Brady and Jill were in control."

"That's conjecture. They might turn out to be more difficult. Nikki at least has a head on her shoulders. I'm not sure about Bret's kids." He grinned. "We could end up throwing the lot behind a Broadway production." Then he turned to look at her straight on. "And how about me? What are my motives to want Nikki out of the picture?"

"Well, to start with, the same as the others. You'd lose a well-paying position. You tried private practice before and it didn't sit too well. Then there are all your treasures you've collected over the years. You spend more than you make and any change in fortune puts all your assets at risk."

He let out a low whistle between his teeth. "You have been doing your homework, or someone's been doing it for you." He changed course slightly. "Do you really think that was a serious attempt to poison Nikki? Paint thinner seems a rather awkward way to hurt someone. The police lost interest pretty quickly."

"Nikki is concerned and that's enough reason to check it out, don't you think? Even just for her peace of mind if it all turns out to be a mare's nest." She paused and flicked some gravel out of her flip-flop. "Give me a picture of that week-end, will you? Where was everyone that morning?"

He shrugged and closed his eyes briefly as if to gather his thoughts. Or play for time, thought Abby.

"I think Tracy and Brady had gone for a jog—separately, of course. Jill was off somewhere with her yoga mat doing her morning thing. I don't remember where Tom was—maybe still in bed; he'd had a few drinks the night before. Kara—well, who can keep track of teenagers?"

"And you?"

"I was having a second cup of coffee in the kitchen."

"So everyone was off doing their own thing and no one can account for anyone else's whereabouts?"

"Irene was in the kitchen. We didn't talk; she was busy planning that night's dinner, but we were both there when Nikki started to howl and yell."

"Did you hear the phone ring?"

"Yes, just before Nikki yelled. That's why she said she didn't swallow the stuff."

"Who called?"

"I don't think we ever found out. Nikki was louder than the phone, so we all ran into the conservatory to see what was wrong."

"Who ran in?"

"Everyone."

"So Tracy and Brady weren't that far away on their jog, and Jill wasn't that into her yoga, and how about Tom and Kara? Were they dressed?"

He thought a moment. "Tom was in his robe and Kara in some weird outfit that could have been pajamas, or maybe not."

"So everyone was close enough that they could have slipped into the conservatory when Nikki left to get her trimmers."

"I guess. But how could anyone have planned that she'd leave her coffee and slip out, leaving it unattended?'

"I'm sure if someone wanted to doctor her coffee, they had all weekend to wait for an opportunity to pop up. Obvi-ously you weren't in each other's pockets for the weekend. If the chance hadn't come then, it would have later."

"You're really serious about this?"

"Nikki is, and that's what counts. What about Bronco and

Irene?"

"Like I said, Irene was in the kitchen with me. She would have been there while Nikki left her coffee. No, wait." He thought for a moment. "I think she went out for a few minutes, to the bathroom, I think. So that washes out her alibi—and mine." He grinned as though to indicate he wasn't taking any of this seriously. "But she was back when Nikki yelled. Bronco? I can't remember. He'd have been out in the yard somewhere."

"Did he come running too?"

"Now that you mention it, Irene ran out of the kitchen with me. I don't remember when Bronco got there. I think he came later. That wouldn't mean anything. If he was farther away, it means he had less chance to tamper with the mug."

"Or just wanted to distance himself." But what possible motive would Bronco or Irene have?

"The earlier weekend, the one where Nikki's car nearly got hit by a boulder. Where was everyone that morning?"

"Now she can't seriously think that was an attempt on her life." He chuckled and then stopped short when he realized she wasn't smiling with him. "First of all, I think 'boulder' is a bit of an exaggeration. It was a moderately-sized rock. They fall all the time from that cliff. Bret had someone shore it up along the curve a while ago, but I guess erosion has weakened it, so it'll have to be done again. It's an act of nature, Abby, not part of a sinister plot."

"Where was everyone that morning?" Abby persisted.

"I don't know if I can help you with that one. It was a while ago and I wasn't paying attention at the time. We followed a bit of a routine individually most of our get-together weekends. Let's see. I remember Kara wasn't even there. That's where Abby was going, to pick her up from a friend's house where she'd stayed over. Tracy was probably in the living room. She'd hurt her ankle and was taking it easy."

"When did she hurt her ankle?"

"I don't know, sometime that morning. And before you ask, I can't remember if it was before or after Nikki's incident with the rock."

"And you can't remember where anyone else was."

He frowned in concentration. "I can't say for sure, but I think Brady was in the den on the Internet, and Jill spent the morning wandering around complaining about her hairdresser. Everyone was trying to ignore her. She is single-minded when she got on a rant. Irene was out doing gardening, I remember that. I can't remember seeing Bronco."

"And Daniel?"

"I can't remember seeing him either. Look, we'd better get back or I'll be late for our meeting. Better not start off on the wrong foot."

He held out his hand to lift her from the step and then stood quietly for a moment with his arm around her before releasing her. As she turned to start up the step, she realized from his grip that he was much stronger than one would think for a man of his size and the only one here who didn't seem to work out in some way. She was distressed at how enjoyable she found the contact. Then a vision of Tony popped into her mind and she wondered for the first time since she got here what he was doing and if he would call.

Chapter Eleven

Neil was the last one to slip into the lounge for the meeting. Nikki got up and closed the door, giving Abby an eye-rolling glance as she did. She was actually enjoying this, Abby decided. Even though she knew any decisions she made could affect the lives of everyone in the room, Nikki was still being Nikki. She'd always had difficulty with empathy and she loved drama, especially if she was at the center of it. Or was she playing detective herself, watching her suspects to see who reacted to her announced changes? She wouldn't get much there, Abby thought; everyone knew before the meeting the direction it was going to take. They probably all had their arguments prepared, but if they knew Nikki, and they all did, no argument on their part would change her mind once it was made up.

Abby grabbed another coffee, her self-deprivation plans concerning caffeine on hold, and took her opportunity to talk to Irene. She paused in the kitchen door, watching Irene stir a pot with a huge wooden spoon. Whatever she was stirring gave off a lovely aroma of tomato and basil. "Okay if I have my coffee in here? Everyone's in a meeting," she added unnecessarily.

"No problem."

"Can you join me?"

Irene looked at her sauce, took a spoon test, and gave

another stir, adjusting the heat control. She got her own cup and sat at the table on Abby's right. She perched on the edge of the chair, not looking as if she was settling down for a long chat.

"I wanted to ask you something, Irene."

She shrugged. "Go ahead."

"It's about the weekend Nikki called the police in when she had the paint thinner in her coffee mug."

"Most excitement we'd had in a long time." Irene seemed to find it amusing.

"Tell me what you think happened."

"I don't know. I guess she picked up the wrong mug and started imagining things. Mrs. Cummings sometimes tends to get worked up easy." Abby noted she still called her Mrs. Cummings when she was actually Mrs. Akerman now and had been for months. Maybe it was just Irene's way of showing her opinion toward Nikki's quick remarriage. After all, it was Bret who had hired Bronco and Irene, and that's where their loyalties would lie.

"You don't think she should have been concerned?"

"Well, Bronco said she's always fooling around with those old mugs. She just picked up the wrong one." Abby wondered why Bronco was the voice of authority here. She would think Irene, who worked in the house, would know more about Nikki's habits than Bronco.

"Is that what Bronco thinks happened? She just made a mistake?"

"What else? The police seemed to think so too."

"What did Mr. Akerman think?"

"I don't talk too much to him, but Bronco says Mr. Akerman told him she was suffering from some sort of anxiety. She got upset real easy. He told Bronco she was taking pills for it."

Bronco and Daniel. Quite the conversations they had.

A quiet footstep and Abby felt the hair stand up on her neck. The only one here who could do that to her was Bronco. He walked up behind Irene, put his hands on her shoulders, and said, "I don't think we need to bother Mrs. Addison with our gossip, do we? I'm sure she has better things to do." He stared at her with cold eyes, unmoving, waiting for her to leave. Abby glanced at Irene and couldn't see the expression in her downward cast eyes, but her body language showed the stiffness of fear.

She didn't want to make things more difficult for Irene, so she said, "You're right. I'll see you later, Irene."

"Irene will be busy later," said Bronco, his hands still holding his wife firmly. "Won't you?"

"Yes, sorry, but I've got lots of work to do." Bronco released her then and she went back to the stove. Abby picked up her cup and left the room, aware of a menacing look from Bronco rippling between her shoulder blades.

Chapter Twelve

The meeting wasn't as long as Abby had expected. The door opened for an exodus of grim faces with Kara the only one who didn't look as though she was seething with anger or frustration. She looked secretive and almost pleased with herself. The changes shouldn't affect Kara. She was still underage and no matter what happened to the holdings, someone would be managing her financial affairs for her. Abby thought maybe Kara enjoyed the drama and the fact that everyone else was upset. That would appeal to a teenager who felt a lack of power.

Nikki came out last. Her hair was untidy and her makeup not applied with her usual skill. Her skin was missing the glow of energy that made her normally look so striking. Abby tried to catch her eye, but she shook her head and took the stairs. "I need to lie down for a few minutes. I'll see you after lunch." Very unlike Nikki. If her proposed changes bothered her so much, why make them? She had the final say in everything, and she never used to give her decisions a second thought once she made them. Had she changed, or was Abby missing something important? Maybe Nikki had underestimated the effect her actions would have on the others, or maybe someone uttered a few unpleasant truths that struck home.

There was no sit-down lunch. Shortly after the meeting, Irene set out trays of sandwiches, pickles, cakes, and tea.

The unhappy campers circled the table, picking up bits and pieces and taking their plates elsewhere to eat. Nikki didn't make an appearance; neither did Kara. Abby followed the pattern and took a plate to her room. It wasn't going to be question period this afternoon. They were a sullen crew. Abby really wanted to talk to Nikki to find out the terms she had laid down and, more important, how the others had reacted. She also wanted to talk to her more about Daniel and his well-known secret legacy in the will.

She tried to nap, but her mind was in too high a gear. She grabbed her runners and waterproof jacket. It looked like rain. It was as good a chance as any to walk the island and make a phone call home. Talking to Mandy would restore a feeling of normality.

When she ran downstairs, they had all scattered. The house looked and sounded empty. She took the path Nikki had taken her on yesterday—was it only yesterday? And half walked, half jogged along the path. She wasn't as freakish about exercise as the clan was, but a little spike in heart rate sometimes made the brain work better. She passed the old dock and the path to the original cabin. As she came to the point, she looked out across the lake. She tried to guess the direction of Massacre Island. *What a gruesome history,* she thought. *They never taught us that bit in school. I'm sure I'd remember if they did.*

She spread her jacket out and sat on the ground. The sky was opening up a little and the clouds were thinning. A ray of sunshine or two was trying to escape. Maybe the rain would pass them. Great! Her phone was getting service. She hoped Mandy would be somewhere she could answer and not in the middle of a delivery. She picked up on the fourth ring.

"Mom! I didn't expect to hear from you. How's everything going? Have you been finding out how the other half lives—got them all sorted and sussed?"

It was so good to hear her voice.

"Things are never the way they appear, but I'm sure you're finding that out as well. How's Ajax?"

"Fat and sassy, as usual. How much do you feed him anyway? I've been giving him the amounts you told me and he still comes up to give me that starving cat look. He's very much an in-your-face cat, difficult to ignore."

"He's just trying it on for size to see what he can get

away with. Don't give him any more."

"I guess there's no sense asking you what's going on."

"Too much to tell, too many phone minutes to get there. I'll fill you in when I get home. By the way, writing a biography about Bret was never in the equation, the real one that is."

"I figured as much. You're not getting into anything dangerous there, are you?"

"No." There wasn't much point in telling her she was on a remote island with one potential murder victim and several other potential murderers. Besides, Abby was beginning to doubt the whole scenario.

"How's the job?"

"Great, we're on a farm doing vaccinations today. Then for the rest of the week, I'll be in the small animal side of the practice. I think that's where I really want to be when I'm done with school. I'd rather be neutering Fido than Ferdinand."

There was a pause she could almost see on the other end. "Out with it."

"With what?"

"I can hear you not speaking. We went through adolescence together, remember? I can tell when you're not telling me something you think I should know but don't know how to say. Nothing's wrong with Ajax?"

"No. And it can wait till you get home."

"Oh no. Imagined disasters are the worst. Tell me what's up."

"Well..." She drew it out. "You know Jess has a cousin who's a pharmacy tech?"

"No, I didn't, but go on."

"This cousin works at the same drugstore as Tony." Another pause, but Abby knew where this was going.

"It's okay. You don't have to break it to me gently. I think I've known for some time there was something a little off with our relationship."

A big sigh of relief on the other end. "Well, Becca, that's Jess's cousin, says there's no conference anywhere this week that she knows of."

"That's okay. I suspected as much."

"That's not all. Dana Gardiner, the other tech, took a week off same as Tony. She told Becca she and Tony were going to Vancouver together. I hate to tell you this, Mom, but I figured I'd want to know."

"Thanks for telling me. And don't worry, I'm not going to throw myself in the lake with a broken heart. I'm almost relieved."

That was the truth, she realized. She and Tony had started out great. He was a low key boyfriend—ugh, she hated that term; there should be a better one for after adolescence—but attentive and romantic when they were together, totally out of the picture when they weren't. Sometimes she felt like a toy he came to pick out of the box when he was in the mood and ignored for other pursuits when he wasn't. Not far from the truth, actually. She wondered, though, if he was casting her off for a new romance, or if he intended to keep them both on the go. She almost looked forward to seeing him again, just to see what he planned. It was always nice to go into a situation armed with knowledge your opposite didn't know you had.

"I'd better go, Mom. Dr. Evans is done with his cigarette break and motioning to me. I thought people in the medical profession were supposed to be smarter than that." Mandy was an anti-smoker in an almost confrontational way. Richard had stopped smoking years ago, and Abby had quit when she got pregnant with Matthew and then again during her pregnancy with Mandy. Unfortunately, she'd slipped up a couple of times in between. It was now nearly twenty years since she'd had a cigarette and now she felt almost as opposed to them as Mandy.

"Okay. Love you. See you soon."

She sat for a while thinking before dusting herself off and starting home. The clouds had thinned some more and it was beginning to look like a nice day after all. She slowed at the old dock and stopped where she and Nikki had talked yesterday. She turned some cigarette butts over with her toe. Nikki's Rothmans were there, but also some other butts with darker filters. She tried to think who else smoked in the group. Definitely not Jill—smoking caused wrinkles—not Brady or Tracy either. Both were pretty health conscious. Of course, she'd thought Nikki was too and look at her. Come to think of it, she'd never seen anyone smoke at the house. Maybe Kara. Teenagers had to try everything, and she'd smoke away from the house.

Abby looked up at the road leading to the old cabin and was climbing the pathway before she realized it. She crossed the front deck, placing her feet carefully as the wood was showing signs of rot in places. It must have been years since anyone used this cabin, but then maybe the damp made wood rot more quickly. The door handle was brass-covered and stained. She turned it and it twisted easily. The door creaked slightly as she pushed it, but opened without pro-test. A damp smell hit her nostrils as she stepped past the lintel. It took her eyes time to adjust to the semi-darkness. There was a window in the south wall and one in the west, beside the door she'd entered. Both were dirty and cracked, but not broken. An old wood stove stood along the back wall, a bucket still holding pieces of kindling for fire starters. Under the south window stood a table and two old chairs, beaten and crooked. No other furniture had been left behind. She looked into the northwest corner and could see a dark heap of fabric, possibly old blankets left behind. As her eyes be-came more used to the inside light, she could see the pile take on form of a sleeping bag. *That's strange,* she thought. *It looks fairly new.* She crossed over and squatted beside it. A piece of crumpled plastic wrap and a chocolate bar cover were partly covered by a Styrofoam box. Neither of them looked old or decayed.

A thought crossed her mind. Maybe Kara used this as a hideout when she was trying to avoid Nikki. It would appeal to a teenager's sense of aloneness and adventure. She couldn't imagine anyone else needing a hideaway. It was possible the cigarette butts belonged to her. She thought back to her conversations with Kara. She couldn't remember any scent of smoke from her hair or clothes. But then she'd try to eradicate it before running into Nikki. Or would she? Maybe the idea of flaunting the scent of cigarettes in front of her mother, sort of saying, "Here I am, what are you going to do about it?" would appeal to her even more.

It was a tiny cabin, and had probably never contained more than the basics. Probably built by someone for conven-ience, certainly not to impress visitors. She pictured a cou-ple, middle-aged, loving the lake, fishing, boating, content with each other and a few necessities. She wondered where they were now and why they sold to Bret. Then she laughed as she realized she'd invented them out of whole cloth. The island could just as easily belong to a corporation or a gang of counterfeiters. She giggled a little out loud. Now she was really letting her imagination loose.

She closed the door behind her and looking down at the first step, saw another of the cigarette butts. She turned it over with her toe and noticed it had no lipstick stains. Every time she saw Kara, the teenager had been wearing vibrant red lipstick. She felt a little shiver run down her spine and could imagine a pair of eyes watching her maliciously from the trees behind the cabin. *Really Abby, you're too imaginative. You can't feel someone looking at you.* But she did.

She walked down the path to the trail, placing her feet carefully and aware the whole time of someone watching her. What made her think that? It was more than imagination. Had she heard a noise, seen a flash of something in the bushes? Yes. There it was, a rustle in the bushes. It wasn't her imagination. She stopped and the rustle stopped. She moved on and heard it again. Would a wild animal time his movements to match hers? What sort of wild animals were on the island anyhow? Maybe raccoons, or martins, or muskrats? She bounded onto the trail with an overwhelming sense of relief and began to jog her way to the house, careful not to look back.

Chapter Thirteen

When she got back to the house, she checked everyone's whereabouts. If there really had been someone in the bushes, she should be able to figure out who.

It wasn't as easy as she thought. The house was quiet. She poked her head around the kitchen door. Irene looked as if she would like to ignore her.

"Where is everyone?"

"The men took the boat out fishing, Mrs. Cummings is in her room, Jill went for a walk, Tracy went with the men, and Kara?" she shrugged. Abby noticed she referred to Nikki as Mrs. Cummings, but was on a first name basis with the rest.

If someone had been at the cabin, it couldn't have been Brady, Neil, Tom, or Tracy. As long as Nikki was in her room—and what reason would she have to be wandering about?—then Jill or Kara were the only possibilities. Except for Bronco. She shivered at the thought. He was nowhere to be seen.

"Did Bronco go with the men?"

"No, he's too busy." Irene looked around her as if expecting him to materialize before them. "So am I," she said pointedly. Obviously, Bronco had clamped Irene's mouth shut; Abby would never get any more information from her—not that she had learned much in the first place.

Abby took the hint and headed upstairs. She knocked

gently on Nikki's door.

"Who is it?" came the mumbled reply.

"Abby. Can I come in?" She heard feet hit the floor and pad over to the door.

Nikki gestured her in and pointed to an easy chair in the corner. "Sit," she said. "I've been trying to nap. I haven't been sleeping well."

"I'm sorry if I woke you."

"You didn't.' She grinned ruefully. "I didn't say napping; I said trying to nap."

"Nikki, what exactly happened this morning? What did you tell everyone?"

"What I told you I was going to. What I've been telling them for weeks now. I just decided to make it official."

"You're selling off all of the Cummings assets."

"Yes. I've got some offers on both the mining operations and on the real estate firm. Any other assets are being sold off as well. It's all arranged."

"What was the reaction?"

She shrugged. "Just what you'd expect. They all hate me. They think I'm ruining their lives. No one cares about my life." She gave her best unloved waif look, but Abby knew Nikki was stronger than she liked to let on. And more ruthless. In spite of the woebegone look and the sleep problems, Abby thought a small part of Nikki was actually enjoying the situation. But she wondered just how much thought she'd given to the effect her actions had on everyone else.

"So, what now?"

"What do you mean?"

"Well, now that you've landed the bombshell, that was the reason for this island vacation. Is everyone going home?"

"No. We're staying till Friday—two more days. I want to find out who's behind this and end it once and for all."

"Yes, but will everyone else want to stay now that you've made your intentions clear?"

"You mean they won't need to suck up any more."

"More or less, yes. What's to stop everyone from leaving?"

"They have to suck up a little longer. I'm still in charge of the purse strings."

"Doling out largesse."

Nikki looked at her sharply. "If you want to put it like that. Besides, if someone does want to kill me, this is the perfect place and opportunity."

"So your idea is, if someone goes home, we can write them out of the equation."

"It had crossed my mind. Now, if you'll excuse me, I'm going to get cleaned up for dinner." She was being dismissed. The queen was clearing the court.

Abby hadn't heard the boat come back, so she thought she might get a better handle on her fellow guests from a quick look around their rooms. Luckily, no one had locks on their doors except for the master bedroom.

She dare not try Jill's room; she wasn't sure where she was. Same went for Kara. Brady and Tracy's first, she thought. She crossed the hallway as softly as she could and turned the handle. As she slipped into the room, she half expected Tracy to jump out and yell, "Boo, I didn't go on the boat after all." But no such scenario greeted her. Instead, she saw the carefully made bed. Irene didn't do maid service, so one of them must have tidied the room. The dresser held the usual assortment of cosmetics, along with a brush with a couple of long auburn hairs caught in it, a tissue box, and a half-full bottle of vodka. This room was the only one besides the master that had an en-suite. Natural that it should go to the only couple here. She opened the bathroom door. Not quite so tidy here. Dabs of toothpaste marred the clean sink surface and a couple of other spots looked like liquid foundation. A razor sat in its open case and little bits of beard stubble had not been cleared up.

She opened the mirrored cabinet door and saw that it was full. She picked up some of the bottles—vitamins, mineral supplements, two prescriptions in Tracy's name that she didn't recognize. Probably to aid conception, since Tracy seemed to be single-minded in that direction. It seemed a rather strange quest considering the state of her marriage to Brady. Was she hoping pregnancy would solve their problems, or was Brady just a means to an end? Or maybe Brady was not even part of the equation? No, she couldn't picture Tracy trying to get pregnant with another man's child while remaining married to Brady. Maybe she had just imagined the attraction between Tom and Tracy. Then she spotted the Grecian Formula and stifled a giggle. Brady was only in his late twenties; silver hairs popping up already? What a blow that must be to his ego. Obviously, he didn't try to hide it from his wife.

The bathroom didn't yield up any more secrets. She went back to the bedroom and opened the drawers slightly one at a time. She didn't want to disturb anything. She thought of the sense of violation she felt when she had discovered her room had been searched. Now, here she was, doing the same thing. But for a better reason; she comforted herself with that thought. She wasn't even sure what she was looking for. No one was likely to leave a notebook around labeled "My Plan to Kill Nikki." The drawers just held underwear, shorts, tees, bathing suits, nothing you wouldn't expect. Abby suddenly felt very uncomfortable; looking for evidence was one thing, but this was all personal stuff she was examining, an invasion of privacy. She'd better finish the job quickly and get out of here.

She slipped out and listened for any sounds. Would she hear the boat returning? Tom's room was kitty-corner to Brady and Tracy's, on the other side of her own. She repeated her performance here. Tom's room was cluttered. A couple of his drawers were slightly open, shorts were lying on the chair, shoes thrown into the corner of the room, and an odd sock draped across the bottom of the unmade bed. Like her room, Tom's didn't have an en-suite. His toothbrush lay along the side of an end table, a tube of toothpaste uncovered beside it.

The dresser top held a shaving kit, open to expose its contents—nothing sinister there. One thing noticeably absent was any sign of liquor. Then she spotted it—a tiny scrap of paper protruded from underneath the razor in his kit. She picked up the razor and opened the folded paper. It was plain paper with a heart drawn on it surrounding the number eight. An assignation? She immediately thought of Tracy, but knew that things were not always as they seemed. It might not even have been for Tom. It could have been something he picked up out of curiosity. But then, why would he keep it? No, she was right the first time. The question was, did the eight mean eight last night, or eight tonight, or maybe even this morning? She turned the paper over, but nothing else was there. What did she expect? A signature? Maybe the eight had a totally different meaning.

She replaced the paper carefully and checked the dresser drawers. Finding nothing of interest there, she turned her attention to the laptop sitting invitingly on the dresser. She opened it. While she waited for it to power on, she browsed the drawers in the end table. Nothing. What a boring lot they were. The screen on the laptop opened up to a background of African veldt. As she expected, there was no Internet connection available, but she clicked on his e-mail folder. Password required, of course. She had neither the time nor the knowledge to try to figure it out, so she clicked around in his documents. She found one labeled simply and informatively, "Plane Crash." Wonder of wonders, none of his documents were protected. He probably didn't expect his sister-in-law's nosy guests to be rummaging around in his possessions. The crash file was a report by a private detective Tom had hired She began to read.

She was so engrossed in what she was reading she nearly missed the sounds of the crew returning. She jumped, powered off, and closed the laptop, slipping it back on the dresser where it belonged. She poked her head out the door. The hallway was empty, but she heard steps heading for the stairs. She closed the door as quietly and quickly as she could and was standing next door with her hand on her own doorknob when Tom appeared at the top of the stairs.

"Any luck fishing?"

"Not really. We caught a few, but threw them back." He didn't miss a step, opened his own door, and disappeared inside.

She did the same and as she sat on the end of her bed, she realized she was shaking. She hoped he didn't check his laptop right away and discover it was still warm. Maybe he'd realize someone had been checking if he looked at dates the file was accessed. Did people ever check that regularly? It all depended on how paranoid he was. She had nearly been caught, but that wasn't what was front-row-center in her mind. She thought over what she had read in the folder. Tracy had been right about Tom's quest to find out more about his brother's death. The file contained reports by a private agency he had hired to follow up details on the plane crash. He had certainly been suspicious, but the last report she had just started to read seemed to put closure to it.

He had managed to locate the missing pilot, and there was nothing sinister about it after all. He was in Australia, visiting a cousin. The trip had been in the works for ages, but had nearly been canceled when he got sick. Fortunately, it was just a flu that disappeared in time for his trip. But then, everyone knew about his trip; was it possible a plan could have been hatched around it? She wondered if Tom was convinced. As for herself, she had other things to worry about. In all probability, Bret's accident was just that, an accident.

She glanced ruefully at Neil's door on the way down to dinner. She never had a chance to check his room or Jill's. Maybe tomorrow. The thought crossed her mind she was avoiding Neil's room because she didn't want to find anything there. She tightened her lips. This could be Nikki's life at stake, so definitely she'd find a way tomorrow to follow up the other rooms.

After the thundercloud faces following the meeting, Abby expected a strained dinner. She was surprised at the patter of ordinary conversation that accompanied the smothered pork chops, new red potatoes, and garden salad. Even Nikki had cheered up.

"Maybe tomorrow, we'll all take the boat out. Abby hasn't seen much of the lake yet," she said. "It's going to be another nice day."

Neil set down his fork. "We can show you Massacre Island. They have a marker there honoring the men that were killed. When LaVerendrye..."

A chorus of good-natured groans interrupted him.

"No history lessons, Neil."

"Who set him off?"

"Sorry, Abby, he likes a new audience."

Neil didn't seem upset by the detractors, just gave Abby a conspiratorial grin and went back to his pork chops.

"We'll never catch any fish with that many people along, chattering away," complained Brady.

"You never caught any without the boatload, just one tiny little crappie," said Tracy with a deceptive mildness.

"Well, you were making enough noise for a whole crew."

"Then how come I caught the best fish? It was a decent-sized pickerel. We should have kept it."

"Yeah, and you'd do the fileting yourself, of course."

"Of course. I'm quite capable."

There didn't seem to be any malice in their bantering, it was just something they did. Not for the first time, Abby wondered what their marriage was like behind closed doors. Any problems they had didn't seem to spark anger, just indifference.

"I don't think I'll bother coming," stated Kara.

"We're all going," Nikki said firmly. Kara looked sullenly down at her plate.

They took their coffee out to the deck. The winds were minimal and the mosquitoes had come out. Tom and Brady lowered the screen that operated on pulleys and enclosed the entire deck area, giving them the joys of being outside in the evening without the discomfort of mosquito bites. Nikki sprayed around to discourage the ones that were trapped inside the screen.

Jill, who had been quiet throughout the dinner, brought out a small ghetto blaster and turned it on. She left the volume low, so the music was just a background. *CBC Radio 2,* thought Abby. Certainly not Kara's type of music. She remembered hearing a brief blast yesterday when Kara had pulled out her earplugs to talk—definitely not CBC2.

Abby sat on a lounger off to the side. Neil pulled a straight back chair to her side and sat down wordlessly.

"Tell me about Massacre Island," said Abby. "Where exactly is it?"

Neil took a deep drink from his cup and set it down. He pointed outwardly, over the slightly wind-rippled surface of the lake. "There are two schools of thought on that, and two Massacre Islands, one on the Canadian side of the border and one on the American. They're both called Massacre Island, both have a memorial, and both claim to be the island where LaVerendrye and his party of twenty-one were killed."

"Which do you think is the right one?"

He smiled. When he smiled genuinely like that, Abby could feel little spider feet crawling all the way down her spine. "I would never try to guess. Apparently, it all depends on which route you think the LaVerendrye group were taking when they headed out for supplies. If they took the direct route, the American site is the right one. If they took the sheltered route, which is a little longer, the Canadian one is the true Massacre Island."

"Are there no artifacts?"

"Nothing that would prove it one way or the other."

"How did the confusion come about?"

"There are records of the massacre in old journals, but most of the information on location comes from folklore from the Ojibwa tribes. They've pointed in both directions. You know how stories are. They change with every retelling. This one's had two hundred and fifty years to collect embellishments."

Historical stories weren't the only ones to change with retelling. Abby thought she needed to do a little rechecking on facts, and the sooner, the better.

There wasn't much she could do now; better to talk to everyone individually again tomorrow, looking for inconsistencies. She leaned back in her lounger, content to sip her drink and enjoy the cool breeze coming off the lake. Considering her reason for being here, there was a strange feeling of harmony about the group. They seemed to function as a family in spite of their differences. Was it just habit, was it genuine affection, or was someone hiding a dreadful secret? She looked across at Neil and found she was returning his gaze. How long had he been looking at her? He smiled in a sheepish way, as though caught in a transgression. Then he leaned back and sipped his drink. She did the same.

Chapter Fourteen

Abby tossed and turned again. She knew she needed sleep. Her brain wasn't functioning properly, but she couldn't turn it off. Little snips of conversation turned in her mind. "They all hate me," "Estate goes to the kids," "You have as much to lose as I do," "Someone's trying to kill me, Abby," "Kara's my daughter," "Are you here to investigate Bret's death?"

She got out of bed, took a sip of water from the go cup she'd filled earlier and set beside her bed, and paced the room a while, thinking. She double checked the blockade she kept against her door, then set the water down and crawled back into bed to try again.

Sometime later, it seemed like hours, she drifted off.

She sat up in bed with that shocking certainty that something terrible had happened. The sky was beginning to lighten; she looked at the clock—five-thirty. Then she heard the scream, long and ululating, a scream of grief rather than terror. She swung her legs over the bed, grabbed her housecoat, and scrabbled at the dresser, shoving it aside. As she ran down the stairs, Nikki, Neil, and Tom were already there. Jill and Tracy were behind her. She didn't see Kara.

Irene stood, face contorted, staring from one face to the other, then turned and fled back into the kitchen. Everyone followed her. She had thrown herself onto the floor beside the prostrate form of her husband.

"He's dead!" she screamed, trying to cradle his head in her arms. "He's dead!"

Neil was the first to move. He knelt beside Irene, put his arm around her shoulders, and gently lifted her up, guiding her to a seat at the kitchen table, where she buried her head in her arms, sobbing wildly. He sat beside her, turning a look to Abby that she interpreted as a request for help, but before she could move, Tracy sat beside Irene and began to croon to her softly, rubbing her back and shoulders as though comforting a lost child. Neil returned to the group huddled in confusion just inside the doorway.

Tom had knelt beside Bronco and, turning to the others, pointed to an object lying beside the dead man. Even from where she stood, Abby could see that it was a syringe. She remembered Nikki's comments about Bronco's former drug habit. Why would a man who had been clean, for years apparently, suddenly start using again? And why an overdose?

Brady made a move to the door. "We need to call the emergency services," he said. "I'll call them. I think we'd better not do anything until they get here."

"Let's get Irene out of here," said Abby. She helped Tracy guide the stricken woman to the lounge. Since Tracy seemed to have more of a rapport with Irene than she did, Abby decided to leave her to do the comforting. "I'll make some coffee," she said. "Or maybe tea would be better." They always said strong tea with sugar was good for shock, and Irene was in need of something.

Kara was coming down the stairs as Abby crossed back to the kitchen. "What's going on?" she said, stifling back a yawn. "Sounded like bloody murder. It woke me up." She said the latter accusingly, looking at Abby, who was the closest to her to assign the blame.

"Go back to bed, Kara. I'm afraid Bronco has had an accident." Accident? Was that what you called an overdose? "There's nothing you can do to help now. Someone is looking after Irene and the authorities are on their way. Go back to bed."

"Is he dead?"

"Yes, I'm afraid so."

"Well, then." Kara turned and went back up the stairs. Abby felt a little shocked by her apparent lack of feeling, but

then teenagers had a different perspective on life and sometimes hadn't developed the necessary mechanisms for displaying empathy. She shook the feeling off. Aside from Irene, maybe no one would feel Bronco's death deeply.

Tom, Neil, Nikki, and Jill sat around the kitchen table, silent and expressionless. Abby put the kettle on for tea and
set up the percolator as well. Then she sat at the table with
the others.

"Did you know Bronco was back on drugs?" she asked
Nikki.

"No! You don't think I'd allow him on the place if he was,
do you? Especially not with Kara here." She suddenly realized her daughter was not with them. "I'd better go find her,"
she said.

"It's okay," said Abby. "I met her on the stairs and sent
her back to bed."

"Does she know what's going on?'

"I told her. She's better off upstairs."

Abby took the boiling water and poured it into the large
teapot. The percolator was bubbling in its final stages of
brewing. "Will they send a plane or a boat?" she asked.

"Probably a boat," said Tom. "The police will be coming,
as well as the doctor."

Brady reappeared. "They're on their way," he said. "They
asked about the circumstances, so I told them about the syringe. They said be sure not to touch anything."

"A little late for that."

Tracy poked her head around the door. "I'm taking Irene
to her room. She wants to go with the emergency services
when they take the bo—Bronco. I hope they let her?"

"If not, we'll take her in our boat," said Nikki.

"Right. I'm going to pack her things. I don't imagine she's
going to want to come back here."

They began to wander away from the kitchen. Abby
walked out the back door to the garden yard. She noticed a
small scrap of paper and stooped idly to pick it up. It was a
candy bar wrapper—Caramilk, the same kind she had seen in
the cabin. Was Bronco the one who had been using the cabin? Maybe he needed a private place to keep and ingest his
drugs. She thought back to her few run-ins with Bronco. He
hadn't given the appearance of someone on drugs. Surly,
unfriendly, a little frightening, perhaps, but definitely some-

one who seemed to be functioning in the real world. She remembered his hand as he'd grazed past her in the doorway—steady and firm.

She shifted her gaze from the Caramilk wrapper and
looked toward the trees. A sudden flutter of color in the
bushes made her jump. Who could be in the trees? Abby was
sure she had seen a flash of material, not an animal coat.
Besides, it was too high from the ground to be a skunk or
martin, or whatever small animals inhabited the island, and it
definitely wasn't a bird. She started forward, but reason advised caution. Besides, everyone on the island was accounted
for and in the house. She decided to double check.

Tom and Neil were sitting at the far end of the lounge in
deep discussion. Brady was stretched out the length of the
sofa, not bothering to remove his shoes. Jill sat in a corner
chair, flipping the pages on a magazine, clearly just going
through the motions. As she paused in the doorway, Neil
looked up and motioned for her to join them. She shook her
head and moved on. As she climbed the stairs, she could
hear voices in Kara's room. Nikki was speaking in a low tone,
with the occasional murmur from Kara. A much more amicable conversation than they usually had.

All accounted for except for Tracy and Irene, and she
knew where they were. She double checked, just to be sure.
Down the stairs, behind the kitchen, was a tiny suite with
bedroom and small sitting room that were Bronco and Irene's
quarters. The door was slightly open and she could see them
both as she passed. So, everyone was present and accounted for. Then what had she seen in the woods? Could she
have possibly been mistaken? Maybe it was a bird.

"Abby?"

She turned. Tracy was beckoning her. "Irene wants to
talk to you."

"Me?" Tracy nodded. Surprised, Abby crossed the room
to the small settee where Irene was sitting. Tracy softly
closed the door on the other side.

"I'm so sorry, Irene." She started to give her condolenc-
es, wondering just what she could say to this near stranger
who didn't seem to even like her.

"Never mind that." Irene's face was puffy and her eyes
red from crying, but she looked composed now. "Why are
you here?"

"Nikki asked me to come," she said simply.

"Did she really ask you to come because she thought someone was trying to hurt her?"

"Yes."

"It wasn't Bronco. I know it wasn't."

"Someone put paint thinner in her coffee, Irene. And someone rolled a rock at her car. I don't know who it was. But I intend to find out."

"It wasn't Bronco," she repeated. "And he didn't do drugs. He quit all that stuff years ago."

Abby didn't really want to argue with a bereaved wife. She said as gently as she could, "You saw the syringe, Irene."

"That may be," she said stubbornly, "but I lived with him. I'd know. He didn't do drugs. Someone did that to him. And the police—they'll look at his old records and just write him off. They won't believe me."

"Was he home with you all night, Irene? When would he have gone out this morning?"

"He came to bed early, but I woke up in the middle of the night and he was gone. I didn't really think much of it. He gets restless sometimes and goes for a walk. Then he comes back and goes to sleep. But this morning, he didn't come back." Her eyes were full again now and she was struggling to keep her hard won composure.

"Where does he go? Does he ever go to the old cabin?"

"Sometimes, I think."

"I thought someone must be going there. The other day I saw some candy wrappers by the cabin. I thought maybe it was Kara."

"That wouldn't be Bronco's," she said. "He doesn't eat candy any more. He has diabetes."

"Would that explain the syringe? Would it be for insulin and not for something else?"

"No, he didn't need shots. He took some prescription pills for it. It was manageable that way. They told him he might need shots someday, but not yet. But he was very careful about monitoring his sugar intake, so he wouldn't eat a chocolate bar. Once he got off the drugs, he was a bit of a health nut."

Irene took Abby's hand and looked at her directly. Her eyes were reddened from weeping and she took back one of her hands to wipe away a stray tear that coursed down her cheek. Abby wondered again why Irene wanted her help. She had been anything but cooperative so far and even went out of her way to avoid her. But of course, that was Bronco's doing. He didn't want Irene gossiping to anyone. Was it because he had something to hide or just his general attitude of dominance over his wife?

"Bronco came across rough and arrogant, I know, but that was the way he grew up; he'd had a tough life. Inside, he wasn't a bad man. I wouldn't have stayed married to him if he was."

Abby doubted that. She'd known too many cases of wives conditioned to stay with husbands who mistreated them, but she said nothing.

"Bret trusted him. That must count for something. I know Mrs. Cummings didn't like Bronco, but both her husbands did. Surely that shows it was just a reaction on her part."

"Both husbands?" asked Abby.

"Yes. It wasn't just Bret. Daniel trusted him too. I heard him say so."

"When was this?"

"It was the day Daniel went away to Vancouver, just before he left. I heard him say, 'I have every confidence in you, Bronco.' That meant he was trusting Bronco to look after things while he was gone." She dropped Abby's hands and said, "I know you didn't like Bronco either, but he didn't do drugs, and he wouldn't harm Mrs. Cummings, and he didn't kill himself, but everyone is going to say he did. Find out what really happened, please."

"I'll do what I can, Irene, but the police don't necessarily jump to conclusions; they'll check it out before deciding what happened."

"Please," she said again. Then she jumped up quickly and went out the door, half running into the kitchen.

The police boat arrived with little fanfare. What had she expected, sirens? Two men trundled a stretcher up the steep path and two more followed them, one in police uniform, carrying a camera, and the other in a dark suit jacket, no tie with the shirt opened at the top. He was slightly overweight and puffing at the exertion. The one in uniform looked like he could leap tall buildings without breaking a sweat. The two men with the stretcher paused in the entryway and the others went into the kitchen. They shooed out the islanders gathered around the table and closed the door. Shortly afterwards, they reopened it and motioned to the two with the stretcher. In a few minutes, they had Bronco on the stretcher and headed for the boat.

With the small amount of officialdom present and the short time they took examining the scene, Abby had no doubt they were treating it as an accidental overdose. The doctor followed the stretcher to the boat, but the man in uniform spoke to the collected group. Tracy had maneuvered Irene away from the kitchen and they were back in her suite. Everyone else sat uneasily around the lounge.

"I'm sorry," he said. "I'm Sergeant Harrison from OPP." He narrowed his gaze to Tom, who seemed to tower over the others, and always gave off an aura of being in charge. "Can you tell me a little more about what happened?"

Tom looked at the others and said, "Not really. Bronco, er, actually his name is William, was there on the floor when his wife, Irene, went into the kitchen this morning to start breakfast. She screamed and we all came running. We saw him the way you did, just lying there, with that syringe beside him. I checked to make sure he wasn't breathing and then we called you."

"He has a history of drug abuse." It was a statement rather than a question. So Bronco must be in police files from the days when he was abusing. They had done their checking before they came, which was why they made the ready assumption it was an accident.

"Not recently." Tom was still spokesman. "He hasn't used that we've known of for years."

"He quit about the time he began working for my husband—my late husband," Nikki qualified. "He did a stint in rehab and Bret made him take tests regularly at the beginning to show he was clean. We would never have let him work at the house if he was doing drugs. We have a teenage daughter." She flashed a glance at Kara, who didn't return the look, seemingly absorbed in a glossy fashion magazine. Abby knew she hadn't turned a page since she sat down.

"I will need to talk to his wife." Sergeant Harrison didn't look as if it was a job he was looking forward to.

"She's in her room with my step-daughter," said Nikki. "I'll get her if you want."

It wasn't necessary as just then Tracy and Irene appeared, a suitcase dropped behind them in the hallway.

"I'm Irene Federstone," she said quietly. "And before you ask anything, my husband didn't do drugs, not anymore. He would never have done that to himself."

"Can Irene come in the boat with you?" Tracy asked.

He hesitated and said, "Of course, we can take her back and talk to her there. Will someone be there to meet her after we've talked? We don't want to leave her alone."

"I'll come with her if that's all right," said Tracy. "Then I'll get hold of her sister. She lives in Winnipeg and I'm sure she'll come for her. Someone will need to help her make the arrangements."

"I think it would be better if I took the boat," said Tom. He looked at Nikki. "If that's okay?" She nodded. "That way I can take Irene and Tracy over and bring Tracy back when Irene's sister arrives."

An uncharitable thought entered Abby's mind that this was working out well for Tom and Tracy—time to be together without excuses. She brushed it away, angry at herself. Tracy was the caregiver in this group. Tracy was the comforter. Gratitude for her concern should be the foremost thought, not snide accusations, even if they were unspoken.

Tom grabbed his jacket and said to the officer, "We'll follow you there." Then he picked up Irene's bag and headed for the boat, Tracy guiding Irene by the arm behind him.

The collective sigh as the lounge emptied was almost audible. Nikki rose quickly and said, "I'd better see to breakfast. Will you help me, Abby?"

They began to make the meal in silence, Abby beating eggs for an omelette with Nikki chopping onions and peppers for them. The coffee made earlier hadn't been touched. Abby set juice glasses on the table and Nikki got the bread ready for toast.

"I'm not sure what Irene had planned for dinner." Nikki broke the silence. "I'll check the freezer after breakfast. There should be lots for the next couple of days."

Abby looked at her in amazement. "You're planning on staying the full time?"

"Of course. Bronco's death was an accident. It has nothing to do with me or the others. We're all going to be staying." Her face was set in steel. "I'm going to see this thing through, Abby, and you've got to help. I can't leave this island until I know."

"You don't think it's strange that Bronco, who has shown no signs of drug use for years, now suddenly takes an over-dose?"

Nikki straightened from setting the table. "Now that I think of it, there have been some weird-looking characters come to visit Bronco. I always thought he had strange friends, but maybe they were dealers, and maybe Bronco was buying from them. It looks like it. I should have fired him long ago." Abby thought it strange that she was able to write off Bronco's death as an accident when she was so ad-amant about her own brushes with danger not being acci-dental. "Bronco just went back to his old ways, if he ever left them. Maybe he was just conning Bret all those years."

"Irene said Daniel seemed to trust Bronco too."

"She did?" said Nikki, sounding surprised. "I didn't think they had much to do with each other. Still, he'd look on things a little differently. Daniel would only be concerned about Bronco doing his job properly. I had Kara to think of."

"I still think someone would have noticed something if Bronco's behavior had reverted to old patterns, don't you?"

"Not really. I tried to keep out of his way as much as possible, and so did most of the others, the women at least. It was an accidental overdose, Abby. Period. It has nothing to do with why you're here."

And maybe pigs right now are flying over Lake of the Woods, thought Abby, but she kept her thoughts to herself. There had to be an explanation for Bronco's death. It just didn't seem like an accident. But Irene was right. Not only the police, but everyone else was assuming it was. It was the most convenient conclusion, and life could go on—for every-one but Bronco, that is. However much she had disliked and mistrusted the man, he had as much right to life as the rest of them.

Chapter Fifteen

When the boats had left, everyone seemed lost in their own thoughts. Conversation was stilted or absent, but no one moved to follow their own pursuits. Even Kara had come back downstairs and hung around the others. After about an hour of self-conscious silence, Abby decided to take a walk to the back of the yard, to the bushes where she saw that flash of color. Maybe it really was a bird, but if so, it seemed a little tropically colored for this neck of the woods.

She crept into the underbrush, which had all sorts of little needle claws that scratched at her legs. *They'll go well with the mosquito bites*, she thought. The trees opened up and she realized there was a path, not a beaten path, but a noticeable one, etched into the underbrush. A twig caught on her shirt and she had to pull it free, making a small tear hole in the white tee. Looking back through the trees, she could still see the house. No one was visible. They were all either inside still in the lounge where she had left them or maybe at the front deck. The only ones ever likely to be seen from here were Irene and Bronco. No one else ever seemed to come into the back yard—not a gardening lot, this crew, more your hot tub honchos. She felt a pang that no one would be seeing Irene or Bronco in the back yard again. She doubted very much if Irene would be returning to her old job.

Abby began to follow the path, keeping her eyes to the

ground. She didn't want to trip and add a sprained ankle to her list of ailments.

Then she saw it—another cigarette butt, the same as the ones she had discovered at the cabin. She had ruled out Nikki, not her brand, and no one else seemed to smoke. She thought back to last night as they had sat on the screened deck. Not a cigarette anywhere. But then Nikki hadn't had one either and she was a part time smoker. Maybe the same applied to whoever frequented this trail. She hadn't totally eliminated Kara, but even if she were the smoker, she couldn't picture the teen crawling through shrubs and trees to spy on the back of her own house. The butt had been crushed out and discarded. She picked it up and examined it. The burnt end had been totally pinched off—Smoky the Bear had made his point. There was no lipstick on it. Who at the house was a closet smoker? And what were they doing creeping around in the bushes? She could see someone using the cabin as a hideaway for any number of reasons—a place to indulge in a hidden vice, a lovers' tryst, or just to get away from the constant togetherness that Nikki seemed to keep arranging for her crew. What she couldn't see was why someone would be sneaking around, spying on their own housemates. The thought made her shiver. Then a deeper chill went through her. She felt the same sudden apprehension she had felt at the cabin when she had convinced herself someone was watching her.

She dropped the butt and turned back to the house. She was sure the track would end at the cabin—that's the direction it was headed—but right now, she didn't care. She just wanted to get back to safety as quickly as possible. She emerged from the bushes slightly scratched and breathing heavily. The chill had left her and she relaxed.

She went in the back door and, in her room, put some tea tree oil on her mosquito bites and some aloe vera on her scratches. When she returned downstairs, no one seemed to notice that she'd been gone. Nikki was in the kitchen, notebook on the table, making lists of supplies as she checked fridge, freezer, and cupboards. Abby remembered she'd always been a good cook, even back in the days when beans on toast and pizza were the staples of student diets. Tracy and Jill were sitting at the table drinking coffee, no cigarettes in sight. She wondered when Tom and Tracy had returned.

She hadn't heard the boat, but the wind was from the west and would have carried the sound away. It hadn't taken them long; maybe she had misread their intentions. They didn't notice her so she checked the front of the house. Tom, Neil, and Brady were clustered around a deck table, beer bottles in front of them. The crew seemed to be segregated according to sex and drinks.

Then Neil looked up and caught her eye. "Come join us." He pointed to the vacant chair.

"No thanks," she said. "I'd better see if I can help Nikki with lunch." She half turned to leave, then asked, "Were any of you just out for a walk out back?"

"No," said Neil. "Why?"

"Oh, it's just that I went for a stroll and thought I saw someone behind the house on the way to the cabin."

"Not me," said Tom. "Tracy and I just got back a little while ago. Then I went upstairs for a bit, and came down to join Neil for a beer."

"I took a quick swim," said Brady. And indeed, his hair was wet.

"And I," said Neil with a slight smile, "was here by my lonesome until the others joined me. You'll note, Sherlock, that my bottle of beer is nearly finished while theirs is just started."

Abby flushed at the 'Sherlock.' "Sorry, I could have sworn I saw someone."

"There are lots of small animals in the wood, and lots of birds," said Tom. "You probably saw something wild."

"Probably," she said, and left them chuckling at her expense. *I wonder which wild animal or bird was smoking,* she thought. It could have been any of the men. Brady was supposedly swimming alone; he could have just taken a quick dip to wet his hair. Tom could have been there after the boat returned, with or without Tracy. Neil admittedly was alone most of the time. No one would have noticed or cared if one of them had slipped away for a fifteen minutes.

Back in the house, she noticed Kara in a corner of the lounge, her iPad in hand, but from the look of her face, she wasn't getting much enjoyment from it. No one would have noticed Kara either if she had slipped away. One of the dismays and sometimes joys of being a teen was that you could easily become invisible to the adults of the family.

So the person in the bush could have been anyone. Tracy was gone part of the time and Jill—well, maybe Jill had been with Nikki all the time. The others seemed to have dispersed after she had left them. She'd have to check. If so, Jill was the only one who could be eliminated, aside from Nikki of course.

She headed back to the kitchen. Time to join the ladies. It looked as though they were going to be menu planning.

She poured a cup of coffee from the percolator. After a test taste, she made a face and added a tiny bit of milk to the dark-stewed liquid. She usually took it black, but this had been sitting since first thing this morning. It seemed like such a long time ago since that scream of Irene's had brought them all running to the kitchen. Abby looked at the clock. It was only half past eleven. She could have sworn it was afternoon. She sat at the back of the table opposite Jill, with Tracy to her left. The open spot beside Jill had a mug sitting there with a logo reading "I Heart Charms." It seemed even here, Nikki had her own mugs, or maybe she had a stack of them in the cupboard, and it was just a case of no one else using them.

Abby took another small sip of her coffee. Even adding milk couldn't erase the bitterness. She noticed Jill and Tracy hadn't touched theirs either. Since no one else seemed to be making a move, she pushed back her chair. "I'm going to make some fresh."

"Don't bother unless you want some for yourself," said Tracy. "I think we're all coffeed out."

Since she had poured hers as a sort of prop as well, Abby sat down again. She felt like a fifth wheel, the only one here without a direct tie to the family. It made her jumpy, feeling she should be doing something to justify her existence.

Nikki had started to chop vegetables. A large colander of lettuce stood draining in the sink. Obviously, lunch was going to be centered around a salad of some sort. "Can I help you with something, Nikki?" she asked.

"No," she said, still chopping. "Well, yes," she reconsidered. "There's some chicken breast in the fridge already cooked. I'm going to do up some garlic bread to go with the salad. Oh, there are some hard boiled eggs in the fridge. You can devil those if you like. I think there are some pimentos somewhere."

Abby felt better making herself useful. As she peeled the eggs, she could hear scraps of conversation from the table.

"I know we're not to speak ill of the dead," Jill was saying, "but Bronco always did give me the creeps." Exactly how Abby felt.

"It's Irene I feel sorry for," replied Tracy. "She's just so devastated. She told me once Bronco was her first boyfriend. That's so hard to imagine, but then, she came from an isolated community, so maybe she didn't have too many choices."

Once again, Abby felt Tracy's maternal instinct was wasted. Why wouldn't they adopt? Maybe some macho attitude on Brady's part. Or maybe he didn't really want kids anyhow and Tracy was putting in a sole effort. The thought crossed her mind that, with all the flings Brady was supposed to have had, maybe he had opted for a vasectomy for safety's sake and hadn't told Tracy. Somehow, she couldn't picture Brady in the back yard, tossing around a ball with the kids. He seemed to share with Jill the family attribute of self-absorption. Tom, on the other hand, she could picture doing just that. But then, he'd had practice. She wondered how close he was to his grown children from his first two marriages.

"What did Irene want to talk to you about?" Tracy was direct in her question.

Abby stopped peeling and turned to face her, wiping her hands on a towel. "She wanted to know why I was here."

"We all know that now." Everyone's eyes went to Nikki.

"She also wanted me to try to convince the police Bronco wouldn't overdose, that he was off drugs completely."

"Doesn't look like it," snorted Jill.

"Why would she think you had an in with the police?" said Tracy.

"I don't know. I think she was just grasping at straws. She also wanted to talk to me about the day Nikki nearly drank the paint thinner."

"What could she possibly know about that?" asked Nikki. "She was in the kitchen."

"No one was very far away, Nikki. And you were gone for a few minutes. If it were planned ahead of time, with the switch ready, it could be done in seconds."

"So, we're assuming the police were wrong, and someone really is trying to hurt Nikki?"

"I don't see how we can think anything else. And I do think there is a connection between what nearly happened to Nikki and what just happened to Bronco." Nikki shuddered at her words and the others looked skeptical. Abby laid down the towel and picked up another egg. "What do you remember about that morning, Tracy, the one with the paint thinner?"

"I told you everything I know. We were all scattered around the house. We'd had breakfast. Brady had been for a run and gone for a shower. So had I. Jill..." She looked to her for confirmation. "She was in her room, I think." Jill nodded. "Kara had missed breakfast and was still in bed, I assume. Tom was making some phone calls in the den. I think Neil was with him, or maybe he was at the computer. Irene was in the kitchen and Bronco was out in the yard. Everyone was there, but no one was there, if you see what I mean."

Abby did. And of course, there would be different memories of the events. Neil had said he was in the kitchen with Irene, but Tracy had thought he was with Tom in the den. "Colonel Mustard in the conservatory with the paint thinner" flashed into her mind, nearly making her giggle. Yet any one of them could have slipped unnoticed into the conservatory to switch a pre-prepared mug. They might have been taking a chance, though. With everyone spread out doing their own thing, there was no guarantee anyone would stay put and not catch them at it.

"So Irene had nothing new to tell you?"

"Not exactly. But she did say Daniel and Bronco had a conversation just before he left for Vancouver."

Nikki straightened. "What about?"

"She said Daniel was telling Bronco he trusted him to look after things while he was gone."

"That's ridiculous. Daniel and Bronco hardly said a word to each other."

"I can't see why Irene would make it up. Especially considering the state she was in."

"Maybe she didn't see him properly and it wasn't Daniel." Nikki seemed very anxious to keep her husband out of this. "Bronco has had some strange dudes looking for him." She gave the salad a savage toss. "I should have fired him long ago," she said again. She looked up as she felt the others staring at her. "Don't look at me like that. I'm not unfeeling. I'm sorry he's dead, but it's his own fault, really. I'm just sorry for Irene." She put the finishing touches on the salad and stood up. "I'm going up to change."

Chapter Sixteen

Abby followed Nikki into her room and grabbed her by the shoulders to turn her around.

"Nikki, something weird is going on here."

"That's what I've been telling you all along. Someone's trying to kill me."

"I think I believe you now, Nikki, but I also think Bronco's death wasn't an accident and that it's connected in some way." Abby let her go and slumped down into the blue brocade chair that sat by the balcony door. Nikki perched on the edge of the bed, her hands clutching the covers, knuckles white. "But there are things going on that don't seem to make sense. For instance, who is using the cabin?"

"I don't see why that matters," said Nikki. "Or what connection it has. I never go there, so no one is going to leap out and do me in there. It's probably just Kara trying to get away from her domineering mother." Abby recognized the look of frustrated parenthood and sympathized, but the time had come for answers to some questions.

"Nikki, you said Daniel doesn't have anything to gain by your death," she pressed on despite the pinched look that was starting to form on Nikki's mouth, as it did every time Daniel's name was mentioned. "But, I understand he inherits Charms, and that's not an unsubstantial inheritance."

"I told you I left him Charms, didn't I?"

"But you also said he didn't know. I've been talking to the others and if they all know about it, Daniel knows, too. Your family doesn't seem too great at keeping secrets."

"Except for who hates me enough to want to see me dead."

Abby ignored the comment. "So we can't leave Daniel out of the equation. He definitely has a motive."

"But no opportunity, if you want to get all private eye on me. He wasn't there when I was nearly poisoned." She let go her tight grasp of the quilted bed cover and began to pace, touching odd things in an abstract manner as she circled the room.

"But suppose he's in league with someone else that was there. Someone that's here now. They could have been working together to give each other alibis."

"Oh, great. I thought it was bad enough that somebody hated me enough to try to kill me. Now you're making it into a conspiracy, and there are people everywhere that are out to get me. Maybe it's like that Agatha Christie mystery, and they're all in on it. Way to make me feel comfortable, Abby."

"I'm not here to make you feel comfortable. Remember, you asked me here to find out who was trying to kill you, and I find it strange that you don't act a little more cooperative."

Nikki sighed and sat down again. "I'm sorry, Abby, if I'm not making it easy on you. I'm just...just...I'm not really sure what I am any more. I've had a relationship with everyone here for years, and I just can't say I've felt vibes of hatred coming from any one. Oh, I know they're upset that Bret left me in charge of the money. I know they get cross when I won't finance their every whim. But that's not hate, that's just family."

"Something else that's weird, Nikki. I'm sure I saw someone in the trees behind the house earlier. I've been trying to track movements of everyone here to see who it could have been, not too successfully, I might add. The men were all coming and going individually, but what about the women?"

"Well, you know Tracy went with Tom to the mainland with Irene."

"But they weren't gone that long. What about after?"

"Tracy was in her room for a while before she came downstairs. Then she came into the kitchen to help."

"And Jill?"

"You know, that's strange. You never seem to know where Jill is." She looked up at Abby with a small smile. "I mean, she's an actress. She should have a presence. But she doesn't really. You know she's there, but afterwards, you'd be hard pressed to say just when and what she was doing. She doesn't talk much and she just—she just is, if you know what I mean."

Abby thought she did, even from the brief time she'd known Jill. She couldn't describe a personality there. She was like a ghost that flitted in; you looked up and there she was, but you didn't know if she'd been there for ages or if she'd just arrived.

"Try to think back."

"She was with us in the lounge until you disappeared. Then she went upstairs to her room. She came into the kitchen after Tracy did. Yes, that's right." She spoke with much more certainty now.

So, no further ahead. For a group that seemed to place a premium on togetherness and went out of their way to stay in isolated locales for the bonding effect, they seemed to pay little attention to the activities of each other. Anyone could have been out in the trees spying on Abby. She had to qualify that; it could have been someone just like herself, out for some innocent reason. Just because she felt chills down her spine didn't mean someone was a menace to her, or even spying on her. She knew her imagination could run wild, and considering her purpose in this visit, she was becoming a woman who jumped at shadows.

"Don't forget to barricade your door," she said needlessly to Nikki on the way out. Nikki was obviously as nervous as she was; the term "jumpy as a cat in a room full of rocking chairs" sprang to mind. She never sat in one place for more than a few seconds and had spent most of the day downstairs wandering from lounge to kitchen and back again without apparently accomplishing anything.

Abby found the bathroom was empty, so she made a quick visit there, stopping to brush her teeth and wash her face.

Back in her room, she shoved the dresser in front of the door before changing into her pajamas. She hoped she wouldn't have to get up in the night to pee. She pulled back the bedcovers and looked around for something to read. She needed a sleep aid tonight. She picked up Agatha Christie's *Ten Little Indians* and immediately set it down again. It was definitely a no-go as a relaxer considering it involved the residents of an island being picked off one at a time, but she found an old copy of Orwell's *1984.* She wasn't really in the mood for Orwell, but it might help fight the insomnia. She plumped up the pillows and slipped into bed.

She nearly jumped out of her skin when a tapping came on her door. She threw her housecoat over her PJs and shoved the dresser back from the door. Opening it slowly, she caught sight of Neil's face through the crack and opened it slightly further.

"What do you want?"

"You are taking this supposed threat seriously, aren't you?" His face bore an amused grin that irritated her while it attracted her.

"There's nothing supposed about it," she snapped. Then repeated, "What do you want?"

He lifted his hands, which contained a drink each. "I was looking for company in a nightcap," he said. "Care for a drink? I promise not to bite."

She opened the door wide enough to let him in, conscious of her unadorned face and her terry housecoat, which was made for comfort, not for visitors of the opposite sex. So much for ditching the nighttime liquid intake.

"Come on in." She gestured to the one big chair in the room and accepted the drink from him. She became acutely aware of the rumpled bed and felt a flush sweep up over her neck and face. She turned away to smooth the covers and allow time for the flush to recede. She made sure to leave the door open. No matter what feelings this man aroused in her, she couldn't trust anyone on this island.

"You and Nikki have been friends for a long time?" He leaned back in the chair and took a sip from the old-fashioned glass.

"We went to college together. There was a group of four of us that hung out."

"If you don't mind my saying so, you seem an odd combination."

"Oh, my family didn't have money like Nikki's did, and they ran in different social circles, but this wasn't that kind of a college."

"That's not exactly what I meant." He paused, considering. "I meant your personalities are a lot different. You seem more grounded than her, as though you have a grasp on things that really matter. Nikki is more—well, sometimes she misses putting people in the equation." Then he added, "Unless she needs them, of course."

"I don't think you're giving Nikki enough credit." Then, with a little not so suppressed anger coloring her voice, "And I don't think it's fair to make judgements about my reasons for being here and whether or not she's using me. I mean, look at the lot of you here." She nearly slopped her drink trying to make a sweeping gesture with the wrong hand. "This little symbiotic group you have here, you feed off each other and have for years. Don't try to tell me it's a case of 'feel the love' between the lot of you. Brady and Tracy make a point of ignoring each other when they're not taking shots, Jill wanders around like an unfulfilled ghost, trying to suck up but never getting the hang of it, the way she did with Daddy. Nikki's jumping at everything that moves, Kara hates everyone equally, except maybe you. Tom's trying to convince everyone he has a drinking problem and thinks someone here killed his brother. Then he and Tracy—" She stopped, running out of steam and wondering just what she should be revealing.

"Well, you seem to have got the hang of us pretty quickly. Maybe Nikki knew what she was doing, inviting you along. Assuming, of course, that she's right in what she thinks."

"It didn't take much genius to figure out. You're so used to interacting with each other, you don't pay much attention to anyone else's observations."

"You missed someone out in your revelations." He looked at her with a steady gaze from still grey eyes.

She looked up at him quickly. "Oh, you don't escape either. You could be out on your own, with your own business, not tangled up in all these affairs. But you're not. You're here like the rest of them because you need each other. You spend more than you earn and you need their help to keep balanced because you're afraid to strike out alone."

"Ouch."

"Well, you started this."

"I don't function well on my own," he began.

"When have you ever tried? Oh yes, I know, for a short while after your bust up with your father. That didn't work, so you found a new daddy." His grey eyes flickered now and she could sense anger in the tightening of his jaw muscles. "Well, you started this conversation," she said. "Don't get upset when you can't lead it around by the nose."

"There doesn't seem to be much danger of that." His jaw relaxed; his eyes were back to amusement. Whatever his faults, he was a man who could control his emotions. Abby wasn't sure if that was a plus or a minus.

Neil got up from the chair and wandered idly to the window, looking out into the darkness. As he turned to face the bed, Abby had a sudden flashback to school days and first dates. She recognized the ruse. She met his glance. *Two can play that game,* she thought. She rose slowly from the bed and repeated his movement to the window. He gave a brief laugh and lifted his drink as if in salute. "Caught out," he said, returning to his chair.

If the situation had been different, Abby might have remained where she was. She felt a stronger physical reaction to this near stranger than she had felt during her whole affair with Tony. Tony had been comfortable—well, sort of, but they hadn't exactly steamed up the bedroom. But, until she knew who was behind the attacks on Nikki, she couldn't afford to trust anyone. She was one up now, though. Now she knew for sure Neil was attracted to her too. Maybe she'd have a chance later to test that.

They were saved from the next embarrassing conversational exchange by a loud scream from Nikki's room. In unison, they dropped their drinks on the dresser and raced to the hallway. Nikki's door was barricaded. Neil banged on the door and Abby yelled, "Nikki, open up. It's us."

They heard a fumbling on the other side and finally Nikki flung open the door and pointed to the balcony. "There was someone there," she cried. "I looked up and someone was on the balcony trying to come in."

"Did you see who it was?"

"No, it was too dark. I yelled and they jumped back and took off."

Neil crossed to the balcony door and opened it. He stepped out and looked around. "Well, whoever it was, they've gone now."

Abby looked back to the open door and the crowd that was collecting there. Tom, Tracy, Jill, and Brady were all clustered with expressions varying from concerned to questioning. It was Tom who spoke first. "What happened?" He was addressing the question to Neil.

"Someone was on Nikki's balcony. There's no one there now."

Jill yawned. "Enough excitement for me. I'm going back to bed."

"Check Kara for me, will you?" Nikki asked Abby. "I want to be sure she's okay."

I do too, thought Abby, *but maybe for a different reason.* She noticed that the others had all arrived at the door in their nightwear, but that didn't necessarily mean anything. Their arriving at much the same time might be significant. Would any one of them have time to have jumped off the balcony, disappeared around the corner, and reappear upstairs in dressing robes in the time she and Neil had run to check on Nikki? It didn't seem likely.

She knocked lightly on Kara's door and, getting no answer, turned the knob. The door creaked slightly as it opened. "Kara?" she asked softly. No answer. She crossed to the bed and looked down at Kara, now visible in the moonlight coming through the window. She looked to be sound asleep, and the low snore confirmed it. Abby watched for a moment, but was pretty sure Kara was not faking and was actually in that deep sleep known only to adolescents.

She tiptoed back to the door. Last thing needed now was for Kara to wake up screaming at the presence in her room.

Back in Nikki's room, she reassured her. "She's sound asleep." Nikki sighed and sat down on the edge of the bed. Everyone except Neil had left.

He motioned her aside and whispered, "Everyone seems to think Nikki had a nightmare."

"Do you?"

"I did at first, but not after I had a look at the balcony ledge."

"What changed your mind?"

"This." He held out his hand and showed her nestling in his palm a clump of mossy dirt. "I found this on the balcony."

"It could have been there before."

"No, it couldn't. Feel it. It's still damp. It's been left there in the last little while or it would be dried up."

"So, what do we do now?"

"You get Nikki settled for the night and meet me back in your room. We'll go over everything together. Besides," he said with another mouth-watering grin, "we still have a drink to finish."

Chapter Seventeen

"Stay with me for the night, Abby." All of Nikki's self-assurance seemed to have slipped away from her. She plucked at the frayed fabric on one of her satin sleeves. She checked and double-checked the balcony doors to be sure they were properly closed and locked. She paced the room from side to side.

Abby gave a quick thought to the man who was waiting in her room, but discarded it immediately. There was a real danger here and having company was probably Nikki's best line of defense. She thought it was unlikely that an intruder would take another chance the same night, but caution was required.

"I'll stay." She was surprised by the look of gratitude Nikki flashed her. It was an emotion she was sure Nikki rarely expressed. "I have to slip over to my room for a moment," she said, "but I'll be right back."

She found Neil sitting comfortably, not on the chair, but at the end of the bed, recovered drink in his hand. He jumped up when she came into the bedroom.

"Change of plans," she told him. "Nikki's frightened and wants me to stay with her. I told her I would."

His expression changed slightly, but he only said, "I think she's right. She needs some protection, but maybe she should have one of us stay with her instead."

For "one of us," Abby substituted "man," but she shook her head. "No, she asked me. I don't think the sex of her company is relevant; she just needs another body for comfort more than protection." She cringed at the word "body" as soon as she'd said it.

Neil stood up and set his drink down. "Wait here just a minute. I'll be right back."

In two minutes flat, he was at the door again. He reached his hand into his robe pocket and pulled out a handgun. "It's not that powerful," he said, "but it will do the trick. I think you should have it for the night."

Abby's mouth dropped open. "I've never so much as held a handgun in my life. I wouldn't know how to use it." She pulled away from the proffered weapon with a horrified look as though it were dripping the blood of past victims.

"It's not rocket science. You point it and pull the trigger. Here, let me show you."

"No thanks, I'd probably just end up getting myself or Nikki shot by mistake. I think we'll be safer without it."

He shrugged and re-pocketed the gun. "Suit yourself."

"Is that thing really legal? Do you have a permit for it?"

"Actually, I do. They're not the easiest things to get in this country, but I do a lot of dealing in valuable artifacts, as you know, and I was able to convince them it was a necessity."

She was about to ask if he'd ever used it, but decided she'd be happier not knowing if he had.

"Tomorrow morning, first thing", he said, "we're getting together and see if we can come up with some rational explanation for all of this. If we pool our information and ideas, maybe we can stop it before Nikki or someone else gets hurt."

She felt a sudden lift of spirits at the thought. It would help to have someone to bounce ideas off of, and there was no doubt in her mind now that a legitimate danger was present. The events couldn't all be put down to Nikki's imagination. She also felt a thrill in the knowledge that Neil was one person she could strike off her list of suspects. There was no way he could have been on Nikki's balcony and sharing a drink with her at the same time.

Abby looked around and decided she didn't need to take anything to Nikki's room. She'd be coming back here in the morning to shower and brush her teeth. Neil followed close behind and helped her shove the dresser a little farther out of the way before leaving the room.

She pulled the door shut and Neil turned her towards him, kissing her with all the passion her frenzied dreams of him could conjure. She wrapped his neck with both arms and relaxed in the mood of the moment. Kissing Tony had never been like this. Neil's mouth left hers and began to wander across her cheek, her throat, her neck. She arched her back as she pulled herself as close to him as she could. Then, as she blinked her eyes, she was staring straight at Nikki's door, which was opened just a crack.

Neil felt the change in her body posture and pulled back, cupping her face with both hands and staring deeply into her eyes. "You're right," he said, "as much as I hate to admit it. Look after Nikki and I'll see you in the morning." He frowned. "I don't like to leave you alone, but I don't think anyone is going to try to get in again tonight. If you hear or see anything that troubles you in the slightest, I'm only a door away. I'll be there in seconds if you yell. But don't open that door to the balcony no matter how much you want fresh air."

She shuddered a little and said, "Not much chance. I'm nearly as spooked as Nikki. We're not going to send out invitations."

Neil smiled and added. "We always seem to be left with unfinished business, don't we? But next time, we're not going to leave it unfinished."

He quickly entered his own room without a backward glance. Abby considered Nikki's slightly open door and paused for a couple of minutes in the hallway to compose herself. She could feel the warmth in her face and knew she was as flushed as a school girl after her first kiss. That's what it had felt like— a first kiss, full of all the wonderment and joy in the discovery of a whole new world. The last time she had felt like that had been when she had first met Richard.

She had to put everything out of her mind except the task at hand, but it was going to be difficult. Abby knew she wasn't going to sleep tonight. That was probably as well, considering her job as watchdog.

"There you are," Nikki said a little ungraciously. "What took you so long?'

Assuming it was a rhetorical question, Abby double-checked the doors and window and started to slide into the near side of the bed, where she would be between Nikki and the doors.

"Oh, not that side," said Nikki. "Sorry," she went on. "It's just I'm used to sleeping there. Daniel always takes the far side. Besides, I'm starting to get up in the night to go to the bathroom, so it's handier. The inconveniences of aging."

Abby was aware of this same inconvenience, but was surprised to hear Nikki admitting to a weakness, especially one related to age.

She slipped into bed after doing another double-check of the doors. *Getting a little obsessive compulsive, Abby?* Nikki's nighttime routine took more time than Abby's, but she sighed and admitted Nikki had more to look after. Which brought her thinking in a convoluted way to Neil, not that he had left her thoughts much. She wondered just what it was he saw in her—a woman of mature years approaching her fiftieth birthday, not quite as svelte as she should be, unremarkable face, though still fairly unlined in spite of her haphazard nightly beauty routine. She searched for an ulterior motive in his attentions and could find none. *Well,* she thought, *here I am, a middle-aged woman and still as lacking in self-confidence when it comes to the opposite sex as I was in college.* She figuratively shrugged off her skepticism, lifted her chin as well as she could in a prone position, and decided to accept Neil's interest at face value. Then she thought of Tony and her struggle for self-confidence took a nose dive. *Why should it bother me? I've lost all feelings I had for Tony, and I think they were just about gone before I found out about his out of town trip.* She pushed him out of her mind and began to think of the inhabitants of this strange island ménage.

Even knowing their faults as she now did, she couldn't see any of the others plotting to kill Nikki. They were too intertwined in their needy lives to want to make sudden changes. Angry though they may be when Nikki chose to disregard their requests, would they really do better without her? Tom seemed too genuinely concerned about the circumstances of his brother's death and his burgeoning romance with Tracy to want to change the status quo. Any argument for Tom was naturally transferrable to Tracy. Besides, Abby couldn't picture Tracy, whom she had come to respect in spite of her questionable romantic inclinations, deliberately harming anyone. It wasn't in her character make-up. And, it didn't look as though her marriage to Brady was going to last much longer. She wondered what would happen when she and Tom went public about their feelings for each other. Of course, it was possible that Brady knew. It might not bother him much since he was usually out trolling for his own diversions. Abby wondered what Tom's opinion was on fatherhood at his age. He already had grown children that didn't seem to be much a part of his life. Was he excited at the thought of potential late life fatherhood? Or just taking it as part of the package of a life with Tracy? If the problems with conception lay with Brady, maybe Tracy was already pregnant. That would certainly start things moving. Maybe her first thought was correct and Brady had done something to prevent pregnancy. If Tracy found out, she might think herself justified in finding a way around it. But then why didn't Brady and Tracy just end their marriage? It didn't seem to be working for either of them. Was she wrong about Tracy and she was actually a gold digger waiting for Brady to inherit before divorcing him? Did Brady use marriage as a cover to prevent other serious relationships? Abby gave up trying to understand. She hadn't been that good at figuring out her own marriage let alone someone else's.

Brady was self-centred, and while she could see him easily discounting the value of another life that stood in his way, she couldn't see the point. The same was true of Jill. Both children had grown into narcissistic adults, concerned mainly with their own needs, but would Nikki's death really benefit them in the long run? It would give them an inheritance outright, but neither of them had the ability to manage finances and it would likely be gone shortly. Of course, maybe they had inflated ideas of their own financial virtues and thought they could manage the money better themselves. But, Nikki didn't really thwart them and made sure they had generous allowances. She carried on much as Bret had done.

Kara might resent her mother, but it was a giant step from teenage angst to wanting to murder a parent.

Which brought her to Neil. She smiled at the thought that she could now discount him as a suspect. No way could he be responsible for the balcony escapade—unless he had a co-conspirator? The thought stopped her cold for a moment, because she had earlier thought about a conspiracy of two.

No, she decided; that was a non-starter.

Nikki slipped into the other side of the bed. "Remember the sleepovers we had in residence? The four of us would find a bottle of vodka, giggle half the night, and then all crash in the one room. I had to hide in case the Residence Dean showed up because I wasn't even supposed to be in Res. My parents rarely missed me, though."

"We had some great times, but I can remember a few not-so-great hangovers in the mornings. Trying to stay awake in Philosophy class wasn't the easiest thing. Professor Ensworth had that droning voice and he was the most boring Professor I ever had. It didn't help he was first thing in the morning."

"I never took Philosophy."

"Lucky you. I only took it first year. I could remember I still didn't know what I was going to do with my life. I think I only majored in English because I couldn't think of another option. Then Education seemed a short step from there."

"I always wanted Fine Arts. My ideal job was to be the curator of a great museum, like the Tate or the Met. Big dreams, eh?"

"Big dreams. Imagine if we could have looked ahead then and seen what we had coming."

"We'd have doubled on the vodka, that's for sure."

"I can't complain about most of it. Richard and I had a good marriage—for the first few years. I wouldn't have wanted to miss that. And the kids, of course. I'd never wish away my kids."

"There are times when I could wish away mine."

"That's only because she's a teenager. Wait a couple of years; you'll be best friends." Abby smiled at the thought of Mandy's transformation from sparring partner to confidante.

Nikki's response to that was an unflattering snort. "By the time Kara and I are friends, she'll be deciding what Care Home to send me to." She went on. "I did have good years with Bret. I know the gossips liked to talk about our fights. Unfortunately, we aired our dirty linen in public, but we always made up. I really did love him, you know." This last was said with a determination that sounded like an attempt to convince herself, but Abby believed her. As much as Nikki loved anyone, she had loved Bret. She was sure Kara came out a poor second and she wondered if it had always been like that. She felt a surge of sympathy for what must have been a lonely childhood.

"I'm grateful you came," Nikki said. "After all those years out of touch, I wasn't sure you would."

"I almost didn't. I wasn't going to. But—well, how could I turn down an invitation for this? Murder and mayhem." She laughed. "That was the name of the play we did for Lit Night our last year."

"And you were the detective even then."

"If I remember the play correctly, I think I was wrong most of the time."

"You're here now and that's what counts."

"I guess we'd better try to get some sleep."

They each rolled over in their own thoughts, hoping morning wasn't too far away.

Chapter Eighteen

Abby woke to a pale light crossing the bed. She tried to catch the fleeting fragments of an unsettling dream she'd had. Although she'd gone to sleep thinking only of the puzzle of who was trying to harm Nikki, she had no recollection of the situation in her dreams. Instead, her dream had involved mountain climbing and her fear of heights. She remembered falling down a cliff and catching on a shrub, then falling again. Over and over, she fell and was saved. So much for dreams solving your problems while you sleep. She tried to capture the rest, but it slipped further away. She had a hazy feeling that Neil had been somewhere in her dream, but she couldn't grasp the picture. She looked at her watch, but the light wasn't enough for her to make out the hands. She really should get an illuminated digital, but this watch was an old one, a present from Richard in happier times, and she couldn't bear to part with it. She squinted at the clock across the room and thought it was saying five o'clock, but it might be six.

Too late to go back to sleep. The summer sun was already coming up. Besides, she had to go to the bathroom. She tried to postpone it, but the urgency was too much. She slipped quietly out from the covers, watching Nikki's face, but she appeared to be deep in sleep. She wanted to get to her own room instead of using the en-suite, but she didn't want to leave Nikki alone and vulnerable in sleep. She grabbed a tall, thin vase and took it with her. Pulling the dresser as close to the door as possible, still leaving her room to slip out, she knelt on the outside to tug at the leg, inching it closer to the door. With just room for her hand left, she set the vase at a precarious position on the dresser edge and pulled the door shut. It wouldn't keep a determined person out long, but would do as a burglar alarm if someone pushed against the door.

The hallway was empty and silent. She had a pee and washed her face.

As long as she was up, she might as well get dressed. She pulled on her tan slacks. She'd change to shorts later if it was as hot as yesterday. As she dressed, she tried to piece together the fragments of the puzzle and realized there was one piece of information she needed. Who could she ask? There was no sense trying to ask Nikki; besides, she'd be the last to know. She thought of Mandy, who would be up early for work. She could call her and ask her to make a phone call to get the required information. Then she'd either be able to eliminate that avenue of investigation or she'd have her answer. She went over the rest of her mental notes as she finished dressing. It would fit with everything that had happened—the rolling rock, the paint thinner, the death of Bronco. It was too much of a coincidence to think Bronco's death wasn't related. She remembered how adamant Irene had been that he wasn't back on drugs. Surely his wife would know? Irene was besotted by her husband, but didn't seem blind to his faults, so she could well be right.

She needed to call Mandy before she left for work. She scribbled a note on a scrap of paper, *"Gone to make a phone call. Back in a few minutes."* She hesitated a moment, then added the time. She didn't want to cause an uproar if Nikki woke to find her gone without explanation. She opened Nikki's door a crack so as not to dislodge the vase and dropped the note onto the dresser. She felt more secure in leaving Nikki alone now that the sun was up. If anyone wanted to harm Nikki, they would have done it under cover of darkness; it was fully daylight now. Strange how people felt so much safer when they could see approaching danger in the light. Besides, she was only going to be gone fifteen minutes.

The morning was cool and crisp; she was glad she'd thrown a sweater over her tee. She tried to sort out facts as she walked, but her brain wouldn't categorize them for her. She needed to sit down with a notepad and try to figure out what fit and what didn't.

She remembered Irene telling her about the paint thinner weekend, about Bruno and Daniel having a secretive and seemingly amicable meeting, then shaking hands as if on a deal. Then Daniel had left before the incident. He had a strange ability to absent himself at crucial times. She wondered again about the relationship between Nikki and Daniel. Nikki wouldn't listen to any criticism of him, but her grim smile when she defended him left Abby thinking maybe things weren't as rosy as she pretended. Why had she remarried so soon after Bret's death? Nikki wasn't the type of woman who needed the guiding hand of a husband. She was perfectly capable of handling her affairs. It would have made more sense if she had played the field for a while. But then love never did make much sense. They say women tend to marry the same type of men over and over. That didn't apply to Nikki. Daniel was the polar opposite to Bret from the little she knew of both men.

The sky was clear and light now and she welcomed the day. She remembered the feelings she'd had of someone watching her and the shiver went down her spine again. She stopped. If the line of investigation she was following turned out to be correct, maybe she was being foolish setting off on this excursion alone. She should have waited until someone was awake to come with her. It was just that she'd feel silly if her suspicions turned out to be unjustified. The bend in the island was just ahead. In a few minutes, she'd be able to make a phone connection and call Mandy to do some checking for her. She wouldn't go as far as the cabin if she could make contact earlier; that's where she had felt as though she were being watched. She was right out in the open on the pathway, so surely no one could surprise her here. Besides, she hadn't told anyone her suspicions, so she wasn't a threat. It was Nikki in danger, not her.

She looked ahead at the turn off to the old cabin and she thought she saw the bushes shudder. Imagination, of course. Abby had spent much of her life conquering fears, but they were phobias, senseless fears that had to be met head-on. It was one thing to learn to step onto an airplane without a dose of Ativan. It was another to rush headlong into danger.

She turned back to face the lodge and stood still to debate with herself. Prudence or curiosity? She thought again about the shudder in the bushes. Cowardice won in the end. She'd go back to the house, wake Neil up, and ask him to come with her. He was the only one she could explain her theory to quickly; the others would laugh at her idea. She hoped they'd be able to slip away before breakfast. Mandy left early for work.

She let out the long breath she'd been holding and started forward with a feeling of relief. She would feel so much safer with Neil at her side, not to mention the gun he carried.

Then she felt the tickle in her back just as she heard the rustle of gravel footsteps. She turned quickly.

"Going somewhere, Abby?"

Chapter Nineteen

Abby's muscles tensed for flight and her brain yelled, "*Run!*" but before the message could connect, the voice stopped all movement.

"I wouldn't try it if I were you. You might be in good shape for your age, but no match for a bullet."

She turned her head, praying it was a mistake, but she looked right into angry eyes and then at a steady hand holding a small pistol. Despite its size, it looked lethal enough.

"Daniel?" She wondered how he knew who she was, let alone that she suspected him. Nikki hadn't enlightened him, she knew. He must have kept up to date on the happenings at the lodge through Bronco.

"Of course. You've known for a while, haven't you?"

There was no sense telling him she'd finally made the connection in the middle of the night, so she waited for him to make his next move. She didn't really think he'd shoot her out in the open, but you could never tell with murderers. And he already was one, she knew now. The attempts on Nikki may not have been successful, but he surely had killed Bronco.

"Come for a walk with me," he said, waving the gun in the opposite direction.

"Where are we going?"

He laughed. "You're not in much of a position to ask questions, but I'll tell you anyhow. We're going to the cabin, and then we're going to plan a little accident for you. Now, move."

Abby debated her chances on making a lunge for the gun, but she knew he would be faster than her. Reluctant as he was to shoot her here, he would if he had to. At least if she played for time, she might have a better opportunity of finding a way out. If only she'd listened to her fearful voice a little earlier, she'd be back at the lodge now, making plans with Neil. She wondered when Nikki would find the note. She'd been sound asleep when Abby left. Would she spot the time Abby had added and start to worry when she wasn't back? Would she call Tom or Neil to look for her? The more time she could gain, the better chance she would have for reinforcements.

She stumbled a little on a large rock sticking out from the path and Daniel grabbed her arm roughly. "Don't so anything stupid," he cautioned. "I don't want to kill you here, but I will if I have to."

Exactly what I was just figuring, thought Abby.

They started to climb the path to the cabin, Daniel poking her with the barrel of the gun as they went. She wished she could feel a little more confidence in the steadiness she'd noted in his hands. If he made a stumble as she did, the gun might go off on its own.

The door to the cabin stood open and he shoved her inside. Her eyes tried to adjust to the darkness of the interior. He motioned her to an old wooden chair that stood in the corner. "Sit," he commanded.

She sat. She couldn't decide whether eye contact would infuriate him or calm him. She decided anything to increase rapport was a good thing and tried to meet his gaze.

Chapter Twenty

Nikki yawned herself awake and sat up suddenly. The morning sun had filled the room with light and she had the feeling something important was about to happen. It was a feeling of anticipation like the one you get on your wedding morning or the start of a new job. She struggled to focus and realized Abby was missing from the bed. The door to the en-suite stood open so she could see from here it was unoccupied.

She remembered the events of last night, and the feeling of anticipation changed to one of apprehension. Still, it was morning and they'd made it through the night. Fears were always more manageable in the daylight. She swung her legs over the side and stood up, stretching. Nikki always rose like a cat, performing a stretching ritual that soothed and massaged every muscle in her body. She wondered about Abby, but decided that she must have woken early and, not wanting to disturb her, had gone to her own room to wash and change. Good. Nikki liked to be alone in the mornings. Bret had always been first up and he was well into his day before Nikki rose, so she was used to having the bathroom and bedroom to herself.

Nikki brushed her teeth and started the shower running. In ten minutes, she was dressed for the day and tousling her hair with her fingers under the blow dryer. She was just about to start her makeup when she spotted the paper on the floor where it had fallen from the dresser. Thinking Abby had probably gone to call her daughter, she relaxed and then read the time on the note again. Abby should have been back by now, but then her mother-daughter talks with Mandy were probably a lot longer than Nikki's with Kara. Still, she wondered.

A feeling of unease stopped her morning ablutions and she went down the hall and knocked on the bedroom door. "Abby, Abby, are you there?" She checked the guest bathroom—it was empty. She returned to Abby's door. She knocked a little louder in irritation. If Abby had come back and then fallen asleep in her own room, without considering how worried she'd leave her...

She felt the presence behind her and jumped slightly.

"Sorry if I startled you," Neil said. "Where's Abby?"

"I wish I knew."

"I thought she spent the night in your room."

"She did. Follow me." Nikki led him to her room and showed him the note. "She should have been back by now."

"Check downstairs to be sure she's not in the kitchen. I'll be down in a minute."

Nikki's eyes widened as Neil picked up the small gun from his drawer and slipped it into his pocket before turning to follow her downstairs.

Nikki checked the kitchen and the lounge, followed closely by Neil. "She's nowhere," she said. "I'm getting worried."

"I'm going to look for her. Check the rooms to be sure everyone's where they should be and then wake Tom and tell him to follow me."

Neil ran out the front door and down the steps to the pathway. He was worried too. He hoped Tom would follow closely behind. Tom was the only one of the bunch he totally trusted. They had worked together long enough that he felt he had a measure of the other man's character. He'd been a little concerned about Tom's drinking habits recently, but he seemed to have reverted to his former self. Neil knew he'd been having a few problems with his exes and remembered how unsettling that could be. He hurried a little faster. Around the next turn, he should be able to see Abby. If nothing had happened to her, that is.

Chapter
Twenty-one

Abby sat as she was told. Daniel looked around the room, searching for something—probably a way to secure her. That meant he hadn't counted on dealing with her even if he was aware of her presence and knew who she was. He hadn't made plans for the disposal of another victim. That was a good thing, she hoped.

An old rope hung coiled on a nail in a corner of the cabin. It was an old length of nylon cord, the yellow faded to a dirty brown. He yanked it off the wall and ordered her to put her hands behind her. She had no option but to comply. He kept the gun lying on the floor within his reach but not hers. What would she do with the gun even if she had the chance to grab it? She wished now she had taken advantage of the opportunity for a gun lesson from Neil. She wished she had listened to her own instincts sooner and turned around earlier. She wished she had never agreed to come to this island. She wished—she broke off in a tiny smothered sob.

"Quiet," said Daniel. "I'm nearly done." He had tied her hands together behind the rungs of the old chair. She had tried to keep her wrists pulled apart to make the bond looser, but he had yanked the cord tighter. Now he knelt in front of her and tied her ankles to the legs of the chair.

"That should hold you for a while." He stood up and began to pace the length of the cabin.

"What are you going to do?'

"Shut up. I need to think. I can't just shoot you and leave you here. Too many questions if you just disappear. I don't want a lot of fuss. It will be bad enough getting rid of Nikki.

Why did you have to complicate things?" He glared at her angrily. "I need to plan an accident." His face relaxed a little. "That's it. You're going to have an accident. I'll have to arrange it somehow so that you'll be found. Otherwise, a search party isn't what I want around here."

I have to stall for time, thought Abby. *I have to get him talking till Neil comes.* But would Neil come? It all depended on when Nikki woke up, and when she would begin to get nervous about Abby's non-appearance. Thank heavens she wrote the time on the note she left. Surely, considering last night, it wouldn't take much to spook Nikki.

"Why did you have to kill Bronco?" she said out loud. "You did kill him, didn't you?"

"Since you're not going to be around to repeat this, it doesn't matter if you know. Yes, I killed Bronco." He practically preened at the thought. "He was so stupid."

"How did you get him to doctor the coffee that weekend at the house?"

"So you guessed that?" His look was almost admiring. "I needed to have it done while I was away in Vancouver."

"Why did he want to harm Nikki?"

"He didn't care one way or the other, really. I just promised to make it worth his while. Besides, I had a little leverage."

Abby looked at him inquiringly with what she hoped was a simulation of admiration. "What was that?"

"Our Bronco may have been off the drugs himself, but that didn't stop him making a few bucks on the side by dealing. The others were too stupid to realize, but I knew." Again, that self-congratulatory smile. "I had a little evidence that could mean trouble for him, so we came to an understanding."

"Did you really expect to kill Nikki with that paint thinner?"

"Not necessarily. If she died, great. If not, it was just meant to set the stage. I was going to be out of town and then when she really did die later, I wouldn't even be a suspect." He waved the gun like a magician waving a conjuring wand and with the same appearance of satisfaction.

"Were you planning her death to be an accident?" She bit her tongue to stop herself from adding "too."

"That was the original intention. I really was playing it by ear. If I couldn't manage an accident, then Bronco would end up taking the fall for it." He smirked at the thought. "He really was an unpleasant man. It would be just what he deserved." *Poor Bronco,* Abby thought, *even his supporters didn't like him.*

"How did you get here? No one mentioned hearing a plane or boat." Abby had to keep him talking as long as possible. She worked at the ropes binding her wrists, but it was difficult to strain against them without being noticed. She thought one of the rounds of cord had loosened slightly, but maybe that was just hope.

"Simple. I was already here when you got here."

"Whoever brought you over is going to say something."

He laughed at that. "I caught a ride with Bronco when he came early to start the generator and get the house ready. And Bronco isn't going to be saying anything to anyone."

"The police will phone the Charms manager in Vancouver to verify you were there. He'll tell them..."

He was starting to get impatient now and interrupted, "She, not he. Isabel and I have a lot of history and she'll tell them whatever I tell her to."

"They'll check the flight out."

"And find that someone flew under my name. Isabel is a great impersonator. She used to be an actress. They don't check ID too carefully on domestic flights."

"So you killed Bronco because he was a loose end?"

"Partly. Bronco got a little greedy and was trying to bleed more out of me. As if I had any to spare. Nikki kept me on a budget. A budget!" He spat out the words. "With all the money I was bringing her in at Charms, she had me on a budget. Stupid bitch!"

"You were willing to kill your wife for that?"

"She didn't think I knew about the will. She kept telling me over and over about how everything went to the kids if anything happened to her, just as Bret had meant. I got so tired of hearing about the incomparable Bret. But it was easy to find out that she'd left me Charms."

Abby wondered about that. Why had Nikki tried so hard to convince him that he had nothing to gain by her death? Did she secretly fear him? But then, she didn't have to leave him Charms; she'd wanted to provide for him. Nikki seemed to have such a need to be in control.

"Enough talk." He pointed the gun at her. "Just shut up. You're not going to be in any position to tell anyone what you know anyhow. I've got to think of the best way to dispose of you when you have your accident."

Abby shivered at the word "dispose." She certainly couldn't hope to appeal to his better nature to save herself. He didn't have one. She worked at the bonds tying her.

"You're going to have a boating accident," he suddenly decided. "You got up early, no one else was awake, so you decided to take the little boat out. Then you fell and hit your head when you pulled the starter cord and fell unconscious into the lake. You drowned." He said this last part with a triumphant grin. "The lake is shallow by the boat house; you'll be there to find. We've got to move before they come looking for you." He laid the gun down beside him, within reach. Then he started to untie her hands from the chair. He noticed the new looseness to the knots. "Clever little bitch, aren't we? Well, it won't get you very far." He gave a savage snap and pulled the rope loose.

"Ouch!" she cried involuntarily. Her hands had come loose with a jerk against a broken segment of the chair. She could feel the sharp pain as a large sliver dislodged and sank deeply into her hand.

"That's the least of your worries," Daniel said with what sounded like a chuckle. He untied her legs and grabbed the gun. "Now move." He shoved her in the direction of the door. She could see the blood dripping from the slice the broken wood had made in her hand. She made no move to stem the blood. *Hurry, hurry,* she said over and over under her breath. *Please, Neil, Nikki, someone, miss me and hurry.*

He pushed her roughly into the trees, moving her ahead of him, gun poking into her back. She tripped slightly on a tree root and thanked heaven it was she who tripped and not him. How much of a jolt would make the gun go off by mistake right into her back? She prayed he had steady feet and good balance. The underbrush had thinned and formed a natural pathway through the trees. She stumbled again, this time into a crevice where a tree root had separated into two. She pulled up short as her ankle twisted under her. She stooped to rub it, but Daniel hauled her up roughly by the elbow and pushed her forward. Her right shoe had come off in the hole and now she limped, ankle flaming in pain and shoeless on the one foot, toward the top of the hill.

Chapter Twenty-two

Neil hesitated at the path division. If Abby was alone, she would have walked farther along to make her phone call. If she was alone, she was safe. If not...he looked down the walk as it stretched ahead along the lakeshore, then quickly made his decision. He turned up the climb to the cabin. He threw open the door and blinked his eyes in the darkness. Only one small window let in the light and it stood in the shade of the large trees outside.

He noticed the chair moved out from the wall and his glance moved to the pieces of old rope lying behind the chair where they had fallen. He knelt at the chair and put his finger on the moist, dark blot on the floor. Blood! Abby's blood, he was certain, and definitely fresh. It wasn't congealed at all. At least it was a small drop. The injury couldn't be too serious. He patted his pocket where the pistol bulged and ran for the door. They wouldn't have taken the path around the lake. Too open. A small opening in the bushes led uphill toward the crest of the island. It wasn't a pathway, more of a thinning of the underbrush, but he could see where a branch had been broken. They had definitely come this way. He pulled off his sweatshirt and hung it on the branch where he entered the bushes. He wished he had a pen to write directions. He hoped Tom wasn't far behind him. He pulled his cell phone out and checked—no service. He didn't have time to follow the path far enough to get to an area where he could call Tom. He had to rely on leaving markers for directions. He still didn't know for sure who had Abby prisoner, but he was beginning to have suspicions.

Last night as he lay sleepless, he had gone over every one of the island group. He couldn't picture anyone in the role of killer. And that near-attack on the balcony. Everyone had appeared too quickly at the bedroom to have jumped down and re-entered the house. No one had been even breathing heavily. Then there was Bronco's death. The drug overdose explanation was a little too pat. He'd seen Bronco often and he gave no evidence of being back on drugs. If no one in their group was responsible, that meant someone they didn't know about was on the island. The only person it could be was Daniel. Sure, he had an alibi for the attempted poisoning and was supposed to be in Vancouver now, but Neil bet that had been carefully arranged and the alibi could be broken with a little checking. He guessed that was what Abby had planned this morning—a call to someone who could prove Daniel's whereabouts. If only she had waited for him.

He followed the natural pathway as it climbed to the crest. They couldn't be too far ahead of him. That drop of blood had been fresh. The branches grabbed at him as he stumbled in pursuit. He nearly tripped on a depression between the tree roots when he spotted the shoe. He knew it was Abby's. He'd seen her wearing it the other night—a blue canvass pull-on. He plundered on. At least he knew he was on the right track.

Chapter Twenty-three

At the top of the hill, Daniel stopped to look around. Abby gasped for breath. The trees hid the lodge and cabin from view. All they could see was the open water ahead through a gap in the trees. She listened for the sound of rustling branches, but could hear nothing that meant help was behind them. Somehow, she would have to find a way out on her own. She swallowed and as she gasped, choked on her saliva, sending her into a coughing fit.

Daniel prodded her impatiently. "Shut up," he said, looking nervously behind them, but no movement or noise rose to spook him. He waited a moment for her coughing to subside and pushed her in front of him again, now heading downhill, toward the boathouse at the shore. The downhill trek was easier on the breathing, but the footing was even more precarious. Abby limped along, looking down to concentrate on her footing and ignoring the branches that slapped her face.

If she was ever going to make a break for it, now was the time. She looked up to see a large green branch across the path. She remembered from swinging willows as a child just how much resiliency a branch could have. She raised her hand as though to protect her face and pushed it forward as far as she could. She ducked as she released it, hoping it would catch Daniel by surprise. She leaped ahead and ran, stumbling down the path, hoping the thud she heard was Daniel falling, and hoping he had dropped the gun.

She crashed down the hill, sticking to the open areas. She knew if she followed this direction, she would eventually come out by the boathouse. That had been Daniel's plan—to arrange an accident there. She would be better off if she could hide in the bushes off the track until some form of help arrived. Surely there was enough cover to keep her out of Daniel's sight for a while. She slipped to one side, in the direction of the lodge, and nearly rolled down a steep embankment. She could hear noises behind her—Daniel must be just a few paces away. A large overturned tree lay across her path. It was huge and dry, probably from a lightning hit. She crawled as noiselessly as she could behind its shelter and hugged the ground, stretching full length.

Daniel was close. She could hear the twigs snapping as he followed the so-called trail. Then silence. He must be standing still so that he could listen for her.

"Abby," he said in a low, threatening voice. "Abby. I know you can hear me. You didn't have time to get that far ahead. Don't make me find you and shoot you. I will, you know. But if you come out now, we can maybe do a deal."

Yeah, sure, thought Abby. *He can't think I'm that stupid that I would trust him.* She lay as still as she could, hoping that none of her body parts were sticking out from behind the trunk. The old leaves decaying on the forest floor began to irritate her nose and she could feel a sneeze coming on. As carefully as she could, she brought her finger to her upper lip to stop the sneeze from forming. Thank heavens, she could feel it slipping away.

Daniel still had not moved. "Abby," he said again. "I'm coming for you."

She could hear a crackle of the leaves as he stepped back and forth across the forest floor, checking both left and right. She thought the noise was coming closer. She closed her eyes and squeezed as close as she could to the tree trunk. If only he would go past, she could run back the way they came and make it to the lodge before he did.

Then she heard silence and a low chuckle. "Thought you could get away from me, Abby? Naughty, naughty." She slowly opened her eyes and rose to a sitting position. Daniel stood with one leg braced on the tree trunk, holding the gun in one hand and twisting a large leaf in the other. "It didn't take Sherlock Holmes to figure out who was bleeding on the tree leaves," he said.

She looked down at her hand and saw the blood was slowly dripping from the gash she'd received in the cabin. She tried to wipe the blood away with the bottom of her t-shirt, glaring at her hand accusingly. Without the blood, she might be on her way back to the lodge now.

"Get up!" Daniel's voice had lost its amusement and the angry edge was back. "You're wasting my time, and yours," he added. "Although you don't have much left."

She had no choice but to head back to the trail and follow it down to the boathouse. He was watching her now, right behind her, so there would be no more opportunities for swinging branches.

They came out just to the north of the boathouse. The last part of the trek was wading through waist-high weeds and wildflowers. The ground was soft and marshy. She could feel the cold, wet soil on her foot, the one without the shoe. It felt strangely soothing against the scratches and sores she'd received along the way.

She looked out at the lake, hoping for some sign of life— a passing boat or plane. Its surface was unmarked by boat wakes and clear as glass, just a slight ripple where the breeze ruffled it. She turned to look up the steps leading to the front of the island. She couldn't see the lodge. It was around the twist in the path and screened by trees. If she couldn't see the lodge, then no one would be able to see her.

She thought of Mandy and Matthew. Would she never see her children again? Never get to hold a grandchild? Would they ever know what happened in her final hours? She fought the rising hysteria and knew she had to find one last way out.

Daniel pushed her into the boathouse and jumped into the small boat tied up inside. He kept the gun carefully pointed at her. Her only hope would be when he started the motor. He'd have to lose his grip on the gun as he pulled the start cord. That would be her last opportunity.

Chapter Twenty-four

Abby tensed her muscles in preparation for movement. In a moment, Daniel would turn his attention to the start cord of the small boat. Her ears picked up a sound of rustling—the sound the tall grasses had made when she and Daniel had waded through them just now. A flicker of hope. Neil! Tom! She had to let them know she was here. Then the rustling stopped. Her heart sank. Maybe it was just an animal in the grasses looking for breakfast. She strained to hear more, but the sound had stopped; maybe it was just her imagination, hoping for a last minute rescue. The flicker of hope died. It was up to her.

She inched closer to the rim of the ledge. She was right beside the boat, could reach out and touch him. He glanced up at her and said, "Won't be long now, Abby. Say any prayers you want to." Then he reached for the starter cord, the gun now held loosely in his other hand. It was now or never. She launched herself into the boat, yelling at the top of her voice as she jumped. Her landing was perfect and her body threw his off balance and left him struggling for balance. Daniel looked up in amazement as the gun left his hand and hurtled across the front of the boat, sliding to a stop on top of the very front of the vee. She stumbled on her sore ankle and grabbed for support herself. Daniel recovered sooner and, now upright, grabbed Abby by the wrists. "That wasn't very smart. You only postponed the inevitable." His grip was strong and she wriggled to escape, her hopes again sliding away. She had to do something quickly. Maybe if she could shake the boat enough to make the gun slip into the water before he could grab it. Then she had a fighting chance to get away. She screamed again, hoping somehow the slight wind would carry her voice to the lodge.

She became aware suddenly that Daniel's grip was loosening on her wrists and she took advantage to pull free, landing with a thump on the floor of the back of the boat. Her back slammed against one of the cross-boards. Just another sore body part to add to her growing list, but all pain was lost in her joy at the sight above her on the decking.

"You!" The word burst from Daniel's mouth like an expletive. She looked up at Neil standing on the edge of the landing with a gun in his hand.

"Don't move, Daniel. I'm not alone. Tom and Brady are right behind me. I'm afraid you'd better give up now." Daniel glared at Neil and looked around as though for an escape route. Neil gave the gun in his hand a little dip of warning as he returned Daniel's gaze. Then he held out his free hand toward Abby to help her out of the boat. She shook it off, not wanting to distract him from his concentration on Daniel or risk pulling him off balance.

She scrambled onto the landing beside Neil and looked up at him. "What took you so long?"

Chapter 25

Neil looked down at Abby's face. Her cheeks were streaked with tears and soil from the ground where she had lain in hiding. Her hair was in clumps with twigs sticking out at odd angles and she had one bare foot. Her shirt was torn and shredded from the branches that had grabbed her and she still oozed blood from the gash on her wrist.

He laughed out loud in relief. "You are beautiful," he said.

Then, to prove his earlier words true, Tom and Brady came pounding into the boathouse to stare at the tableau before them. "Haul him out of the boat," Neil said, motioning to Brady. "He's been on the island all the time, and if I'm not mistaken, he's also responsible for Bronco's death as well as the attacks on Nikki."

Daniel's body slumped and his cocky attitude deserted him. He willingly let Tom pull him out of the boat and made no resistance as they prodded him up the hill to the lodge.

"Oh, Neil, I think I'd better go ahead," said Abby, as she pushed past them on the path, being sure to keep a wide berth from Daniel.

"Sure. You need to lie down. And get those cuts looked at too."

"It's not that. I just want to get to Nikki before she sees us all parading into the lodge." With that comment thrown over her shoulder, she hobbled as fast as she could with one shoe missing. Nikki was waiting on the front deck.

"What in the world has happened to you?" Nikki jumped up and ran to her. "Where are the guys? Did they catch up to you? You'd better put some disinfectant on that hand. Did you fall?"

By the time she'd managed to stop the flow of Nikki's questions, it was too late to prepare her. Nikki was looking over her shoulder and could see the procession coming up the path. She sat down quickly as her complexion paled. It was like watching the kid bouncer in her neighbors' yard deflate. She just sank into a lump. Abby sat beside her and put her arms around her. "Let's go inside, Nikki. I'll tell you all about it," she said gently.

Abby and Nikki sat on the big leather sofa at the end of the lounge. Tracy had brought them tea, and she and Jill had joined them. She didn't know where Neil and Tom had gone with Daniel, but she assumed they were keeping him away from Nikki and calling the police. Kara was missing, probably in her room.

Abby looked around. "Maybe I should tell Nikki first," she began, but Nikki interrupted her. "No, go on. I think I know what's coming. I just need to hear the details. We all need to know. You know we have no secrets in this family." She gave a weak grin with her attempt at humor.

As concisely as she could, Abby began to recite the events of the morning, beginning with her early morning plans to call Mandy to check Daniel's alibi. She tried to keep her voice level and calm, but a tremor came, unstoppable, when she began to tell of the trek over the island to the boathouse. She skipped a lot of details that Nikki didn't need to know, at least now.

When she was done, Nikki took a large sip of her sweetened tea and stood. "I'd better go see to Kara now, and let her know what's happened. I told her to stay in her room." Without another word, she left the room and headed up the stairs.

Meanwhile, Brady had called the police and Neil and Tom were keeping watch over Daniel on the deck, as far away from Nikki as they could keep him. Abby sat for a few moments with Tracy and Jill, filling in a few details and answering their questions the best she could. Then Tracy slipped out for a moment and reappeared with peroxide, bandages, and a basin filled with warm water.

After her wounds were tended to, Abby went upstairs and changed her clothes. She looked at herself in the mirror and gave her face a good wash. She didn't have the energy to reapply her makeup. She lay down on the bed to rest her eyes, with no intention of falling asleep. The next thing she knew, Tracy was shaking her gently by the shoulder. She sat up quickly, startled.

"Sorry, I didn't mean to scare you. You've had a rough day. The police are downstairs and they need to talk to you. They've already interviewed everyone else, but we left you for last so you could get a rest."

"Thanks, Tracy."

She felt worse not better after her sleep and had to focus on the questions the police sergeant was asking her. She noticed the police officer had a big mug of coffee in front of him and went to the pot to get some to help wake her and clear her mind. The pot was empty. She didn't bother to start a new one; she only wanted to get this over with. The officer was a large man, slightly rounded at the center, and with the shoulders of a fullback, but his voice was kind and soft. He wasn't the one who had come yesterday for Bronco. *Good grief! Was it only yesterday?* But he seemed to appreciate what she had been through. It was harder to tell a story in question and answer format than to tell the story as a narrative, but eventually, the ordeal was over.

The sergeant stood up. "That's all we need for now, but we'll have to get a formal statement from you in Kenora. Will you be leaving soon?"

"Believe me," she replied, "I can't leave here soon enough. I don't want to spend another night here."

He smiled wordlessly but sympathetically. Then he stopped at the door and repeated, "Stop for your statement before you leave Kenora."

Nikki's family might be dysfunctional, but they were a family that seemed to need each other. They gathered together in the lounge, not talking much, but seeming to draw strength from each other. Tracy got up every once in a while to fill teacups, but Brady made the first move to the liquor cabinet for something stronger and soon, they all had a glass in their hands.

Nikki came into the room with Kara at her side. Nikki had been crying; her eyes were puffy, her makeup wiped off and not reapplied. Kara looked uncomfortable and scanned the faces in the room before sitting down in isolation in a large, deeply upholstered chair in a corner. Brady offered her a glass. She looked up at him sharply, then at her mother. Not facing protest, she held out her hand for the glass and took a large gulp, then set it down on the table. Abby searched her face for signs of triumph or satisfaction, but could see none, only uncertainty and discomfort in her slumped posture. She kept her eyes firmly on her mother. Maybe Kara was starting to make the transition to adulthood.

Nikki looked around at the faces and pulled out a small smile.

"Well," she said, "I've never been much good at taking advice when it comes to my personal life, and look where it got me. I guess I'll have to start listening to you all a little more." She turned her smile to Kara, and Abby was relieved to see an answering token smile. Maybe half the problem with Nikki and Kara's relationship had come down to Daniel. Abby wouldn't put it past him to have muddied the waters whenever possible. And a teenage girl living in the same house as a stepfather she loathed was not the basis for a great mother-daughter bond. She hoped things would be easier for them now. Some good had to come out of this situation.

"I think we've all had about enough of this island," Nikki went on. "So we'll pack up and be gone first thing in the morning. The police will have access to all they need—the boathouse, the cabin, and I'll leave them the keys to the house in case they need more in here. Brady, I'll leave you in charge of doing the necessary shutdowns, now that we don't have Bronco. Tom, you and Neil can look after the pool and hot tub. And Tracy and Jill, you can help me look after the food that's left and clean up the kitchen and pantry." She looked across at Abby. "I think we'll give you a pass, Abby. You've done enough."

Abby felt a lifting of her spirits. In spite of the blow she had just received, Nikki still had enough of her old self to be organizing and assigning. That boded well for her recovery. Abby had a strange thought. Maybe there wasn't that much to recover from. Nikki had been protective of Daniel and insistent he had nothing to do with her problems, but maybe she had had suspicions right from the beginning. Maybe that was why she wanted Abby's objectivity—to prove her right or wrong.

Later, Nikki and Abby sat alone in the kitchen over mugs

of cooling tea. The others were dispersed to their own pursuits and the house was quiet.

"Kara and I are going away on a holiday when we have everything sorted out," Nikki was saying. "I think things are looking up between us."

"That's great," said Abby, "but don't get too complacent. Her adolescence isn't quite over and you may have a stormy time or two ahead. If she's like Mandy, it will be about another year before she comes out of the tunnel into adulthood."

"I can live with that. I know I've been ignoring her and I plan to make that up to her."

"Tell me the truth, Nikki. Did you ever suspect Daniel was at the bottom of your problems?"

"Actually, no. Oh, I knew he was up to something, but I figured it was siphoning money off Charms without telling me. I know he had expensive tastes and he was always broke, in spite of the generous salary he got. But I never thought he could really want me dead." Her eyes teared up, but she shook off the emotion and went on. "I really want to thank you, Abby, for sorting everything out."

"That's what friends are for."

"Yes, but not for putting in danger. You were nearly killed yourself, and I want to make it up to you. I'd like to send you off on a great vacation too. Maybe even come to the Caribbean with Kara and me."

"I think you and Kara need to be alone, Nikki."

"Maybe you're right. Well then, how about a cruise—maybe on the Mediterranean?"

Abby laughed. Nikki hadn't taken long to get back to her old self.

"Thanks but no thanks, Nikki. I appreciate your generosity, but I'm afraid I've had a better offer." With that, she stood and took her cup over to the sink. She rinsed it out, smiling to herself, and said, "Well, I'm off to bed. It's going to be a busy day tomorrow."

"Well, I'll be..." It wasn't often Abby could leave Nikki speechless, and she enjoyed the situation.

In spite of the excitement, Abby didn't lie awake. She fell into a deep sleep that lasted most of the night. Then she woke, went to the bathroom, and fell asleep again.

Next morning, she called Mandy. She paced the path just

past the cabin and felt only a slight shudder as she looked up the steps to where she had nearly lost her life.

"Do you think you can look after Ajax for another few days?"

"I'd be happy to. And I mean that sincerely."

"Things still not going well in the roommate department?'

"Actually, they're going very well, from my point of view anyway. I think Jess needed time alone with her boyfriend to see him in his true colours. When I was there, she spent all her time defending him to me. Now, she's looking at him in a different light and I think a couple more days will be all she needs to send him packing. I have my fingers crossed. Oh, by the way, Tony's called a couple of times. Wouldn't leave a message."

"Tony who?"

Mandy laughed. "Way to go." Then she stopped short. "Wait a minute. Why are you staying on? Still problems of Nikki's to sort out?"

"Not really. Her problems seem to be resolved, at least for now. The story's too long to go into till I get home. I'm actually getting ready to leave the island. But I'm making a stop on the way home." Before Mandy could ask any more questions, she said, "Uh, oh. I think I'm about to lose the signal. Talk to you later. Thanks for doing this, Mandy." She hung up and waved to Neil who was beckoning to her at the bend in the trail.

"Hurry up," she could hear. "The plane's leaving."

Abby settled herself into the plane beside Neil and felt the familiar churning in her stomach as it began to taxi. Neil squeezed her hand and said, "It's just a short hop. We'll be there in minutes."

"It's funny, but it's only the take-offs and climbs that bother me. I'm not too bad once we're level. Landings are great. I just love to see that ground or water coming up to meet me."

"Did you tell your daughter where you were going?"

"Not exactly."

"Or who with?"

"Not exactly."

He laughed. "We'll have plenty of time for that."

About the Author

Sharon McGregor is a prairie author who has recently transplanted to the west coast. She has written many humor, romance and mystery stories for magazines. She has several romance novellas in the process of publication but mystery is her genre of choice. When not fighting with her cat Zoey for control of the computer keyboard, she is working at her ice cream shop.

www.ingramcontent.com/pod-product-compliance
Lightning Source LLC
Chambersburg PA
CBHW030537130626
46552CB00006B/2302